Ball(s) is a work of fiction. Names, characters, places, and incidents are the products of the author's imagination and are used fictitiously. Any resemblance to actual events, locations, persons—living or dead—is entirely coincidental.

Published in the United States by Beach Hooch Books.

Ball(s)

A Novel

by

LEW HOLTON

BEACH HOOCH BOOKS  Murrells Inlet, SC

Chapter 1

Spring 2001, not all of the new growth in the Virginia Tidewater was as welcome as the crocuses and the dogwood blooms.

"It's called an orchiectomy. It involves the surgical removal of the testicles."

Casey Frye felt suddenly as if he were sweating ice water, and the doctor's voice sounded distant and tinny like it was coming from an old TV in another room down a long linoleum hall.

"There is a high success rate with this kind of procedure, and there is every reason to believe you're going to come through this fine. You're very lucky."

For a moment, the mental meltdown image of Munch's *The Scream* floated in stunned silence across the empty room that his mind had become, and then the voices in Casey's head assembled themselves into an ugly, shouting flash-mob. "You wanna cut off my *what*?!" "Oh, so *this* is what lucky feels like." "Cancer? *Cancer?* Am I gonna die?" "Hmmm...there's a phrase you never thought you'd ever hear—'We're going to surgically remove your testicles.'" "Oh, fuck! Oh, fuck! Oh, fuck!" The only voice that made it through to the outside, though, was more creak than shout. "When? I mean, how long do I...?"

"Your AFP is 255. Normal is about 3. The ultrasound shows a mass on your right testicle, and what may be a much smaller, but still disturbing mass on the left. If there was any other solution, I would be telling you about it right now. You know that, right?"

"But both? The right one I understand. I can feel it. I know it's a problem. But both? I mean, isn't there a possibility—"

"Look, Casey, if you'd be more comfortable with a second opinion..."

"I'd be more comfortable if we were talking about something else besides cutting off my balls!" In the meta-galactically quiet moment that followed, Casey realized that the near-hysterical breathing sounds he heard were his own. "I'm sorry," he said. "I know you're telling me straight-up what I need to hear. It's just not what I *want* to hear."

"I understand."

"And I don't."

The doctor handed him several pamphlets and a short stack of papers clipped together.

"I want you to come back in one week. We're not going to *do* anything when you come back, except talk. But I want you to read these while you're thinking about all this, okay?"

"Okay."

"All right, then. They'll schedule our next meeting at the desk."

As he stood at the desk and looked at the young woman who was writing information on his appointment card, he wondered for just a moment why she didn't look him in the eye. Did she know?

Would women, for the rest of his life, avoid eye contact with him? When he got in his car, rather than start it, he just sat there. His mind raced, but it was stuck in neutral. Suddenly, what flew out of the whir was the memory of a story his father had told him the afternoon after Casey had had his tonsils taken out. His father said that when *he* was a kid and had *his* tonsils removed, they gave the tonsils to him in a jar of formaldehyde to take home with him. The image of a mason jar, filled with a clear brownish liquid, in which two sadly detached testicles floated—for some reason, the jar sitting on the living room mantle of the house in which he grew up—took center stage in his mind's eye, and, strangely, he found the sounds of laughter coming from his mouth, while at the same time tears rolled from his eyes, and then they blurred together until he couldn't tell which he was doing. And for the moment, it didn't seem to matter.

Chapter 2

Once you figure out what's going to kill you, you start making deals with it—whatever it is— liquor, cigarettes, a disease, a lifestyle. The negotiations are intense and nonstop. Though you know it's going to get you, you wheel and deal about the when and the where, about the things you want to accomplish before it takes you, about how much you're going to suffer before the end. Since both of you know who holds what would seem to be the ultimate trump card, all you can do is to try to appeal to the thing's curiosity and sense of humor— perverse as those might be—to make the game as interesting as possible for it so that it is willing to concede a few things along the way in exchange for whatever entertainment value the concessions might afford. "After all," you say to it, "once I'm gone, I'm gone." The power of life and death is not just the thing's most powerful trump card, it is its *only* source of real power, and once it has played it— sure, you're gone—but it loses, too. And it knows it. It knows it loses the only thing it ever really had: *that power*. And no one or no thing that has held that kind of power wants to give it up. Your awareness of that is the trump card that *you* hold. Your power is your mortality, your certainty of death.

Woody Zildjian sat at a small table in the corner of the Strike Two, took a sip of his second rum and Coke of the night, and settled into the negotiations with his companions. The casual observer may have glanced over and thought he was sitting alone, but Woody raised his glass to the spectre of alcohol sitting across from him and said, "Now don't get upset, but Smokey here..."—he nodded toward the chair to his right—"...he's made me a cigarette offer that's pretty hard to resist. So...I'm going to have one." He spoke directly to the chair across from him, making no pretense of including the occupant of the chair to his left. Woody knew that Dementia, who sat smiling to his left, would take no offense, though he would certainly file the details of the deal away to bring up at some future negotiation of his own. "This has little or nothing to do with you and me," Woody told Alky. "It's a side deal, plain and simple." He withdrew the cigarette—a little bent, the paper wrinkled but not broken—from his shirt pocket and smoothed and straightened the white tube between the fingertips of his left hand. He lifted the cigarette to his lips, held it there on the right side of his mouth, as he spoke out of the left side. "Tony gave it to me," he said. "I didn't buy any." Tony, behind the bar, was half-owner of the Strike Two. Taz was the other half. On more than one occasion, Woody had been tempted to point out that a bar name that hinted at the fact that a guy with visions of cocktail encounters and amorous adventures with members of the opposite sex was walking into said bar with two strikes against him *might* not be the best promotional idea ever conceived. But both Tony and Taz were good to him, and so far, at least, he hadn't been called out on strikes in any of his amorous-intentions-plate-appearances—though, admittedly, there had been a few foul tips and a couple of games called on account of inclement weather.

The naming of the Strike Two Bar came about in the same fashion and flowed from the same creative font as the one which produces the tagging of a boy child with the profound and distinctive label "Jr." First, there was the Strike One Bar; then Tony and Taz acquired the second bar, which became the...Strike Two. They just couldn't bring themselves to snub the obvious.

The Strike One, at least, seemed born of the marriage of logic and tradition. Only a block away from and with a view—had there actually been anything still there *to* view—of the famous rotunda entrance of Ebbets Field—a magnificent imaginary view, they liked to call it—when Tony and Taz opened the Flatbush bar, the theme of the decor seemed a no-brainer: vintage Bumabilia. The Strike One was Tony's first entrepreneurial venture. Taz had been around bars—bartending, managing, even owning one briefly—all his life. He had learned a lot of hard, but valuable lessons. Taz had the know-how. Tony had good taste, an eye for details, a little family money, and a fabulous credit rating. And the Strike One was very good to them.

A couple of years later, when they found out

that the owner of a corner bar in Taz' old neighborhood of Bay Ridge was looking to sell out and move down south, they acted quickly. And named the new place hastily. Thus, Strike Two. But the similarities ended there.

Woody struck a match and allowed the flame to shimmer and dance just beyond the tip of the cigarette, taking its glow from only the edge of the heat without actually touching the substance of the fire itself. He inhaled deeply and allowed himself a smile before blowing out the match. He took another sip of rum and enjoyed the mix and mingle of his two companions, smoke and alcohol, as he took them both in. For the moment, they were both his—he had them both. Or they both had him. It didn't matter—the sensation was the same.

Woody reached into the breast pocket of his sport coat and pulled out a folded-in-half postcard. He unfolded it and held it within the small circle of light offered up by the votive candle within its frosted glass holder which sat on the table. For a moment he wondered what the candle thought of its job—of its station in candle life. He wondered if the candle had a brother who might have gotten a religious calling and now glowed upon an altar in a church somewhere in the city. Or a sister, maybe, who flickered her life away on a bedside table in a brothel. Where along the candle continuum, he wondered, did bar candle duty lie? He decided that, like most things, it depended on the people you worked for and with. Location, of course, was a factor. There were worse things, he decided, than life as a bar candle. He smiled to himself—*Either way it's a tallow existence*, he thought. For a moment, he was tempted to say the pun aloud, just to hear the sound of it for his own entertainment. But he thought better of it.

The soft light washed over the picture on the postcard and added to the visual trickery that the studio lighting and shadow and angle had contributed to the black and white image. It was a pleasant trickery, though—a come-play-with-me invitation to the eyes. At first glance, it seemed that the camera had captured just the right side of a woman's face—not quite half the face—stopping just shy of the nose—the right eye, the cheekbone, a wisp of hair along the temple—the face in the midst of tilting upward, the muscle play of the cheek suggesting a smile on the unseen lips. But upon a more attentive viewing, the impulses along the optic nerve were re-routed to a more libido-rich neighborhood within the brain, and one's eyes realized that they were being offered not just a casual glance at a passing face, but a more intimate and voyeuristic invitation. The vase-like curve down the center of the picture was not cheek at all, but the smooth line of a woman's back from shoulder to slender waist—right-profiled with just a slight twist away from the viewer. What had first seemed to be an eye was shadow playing in the hollow created as the flute of her neck met the smooth furrow along the top of her collarbone, drawn into an almond-shaped darkened recess by the turning away of her head. There was no wisp of hair along the temple; there was instead just a sliver of her left arm as it lifted her long dark hair off the back of her neck and pulled the hair aside so that it undoubtedly fell into the V formed by the unseen side of her neck and her raised, upstage arm. It was the view one would have of her, Woody imagined, if you stood behind her in a darkened room and watched her as she stood before an uncurtained window bathed in the light of a full moon. He wondered then who the pose was for—for he who stood behind her, or for whoever stood in the darkness beyond the window? The caption beneath the picture read, "Self Portrait Photography by Merilee Mikatitis." Woody had known immediately that Merilee Mikatitis was a woman he wanted to meet.

Woody looked over at the bar, at the several patrons who sat and pondered their drinks, at the one couple who seemed to be wending their way through the small talk of a first date, at Mack who sat watching the hockey game on the TV over the bar. Mack was a regular—a former musician who had settled into the straight life of managing equipment and vehicles for a large construction company. It had been easy to identify Mack as a former musician—a drummer, in fact—because after the initial introduction he had asked—as they always did—"Zildjian? Oh, yeah? Like the cymbals?" "Yeah," Woody had answered, "like the cymbals. But no relation—that I know of." At one point Woody had entertained a brief glimmer of interest in doing the genealogical research, just to see where the connection was. He figured there almost had to be a connection. There were not a lot of Zildjians in the phone book. Any phone book. But the glimmer of interest had winked out almost as quickly as it had appeared. He knew the name was Turkish, but the family had been here so long and any sense of ethnicity had been so diluted by the mongrelization produced by the marriages of ancestors with Irish and English and Italian and German descendants that the name—though nicely distinctive—conjured up no Old World images at all—not for him, anyway. At least that's what he'd decided. He was as American as network news. It had been only a few years ago that he had even become aware that Turkey was the home of Troy. For some reason he couldn't quite get a handle on, the idea of a connection with Troy was an interesting idea to entertain. Troy. Helen of Troy. The Trojan Horse. Trojan condoms. Something in the mix of beautiful women, sexuality, and subterfuge had an enticing feel to it.

A group came through the door of the bar—four women, two men. Two of the women were dark-haired and petite. Either could be the artist—the woman in the photo. About a dozen frames of different sizes were displayed along the walls—each draped with a piece of black fabric. Woody looked back at the postcard and read again the smaller print at the bottom of the card: "Opening—8pm, Thurs., March 8th, 2001—Strike Two Bar & Galleria, 7910 3rd Ave., Brooklyn. Music by David Ezell. Complimentary wine 8-10 pm." It must be almost eight, he thought, without looking at his watch. For a moment, he imagined himself going up to the bar and saying to Tony, "I'll have a glass of your very best complimentary wine for the unveiling." "Ah, yes," Tony would reply, "this is an excellent year for complimentary wine. A bit honeyed perhaps, but I think you'll be amused by its flattery." His rum and Coke clinked its ice against the side of the glass to get his attention. "Don't even think about it," whispered the rum. The Coke just floated there with a fizzy look on its face.

   Woody took the last draw from his cigarette and rose from his chair. Taking his drink with him, he walked over and stood before the first of the draped frames on the wall. He closed his eyes and waited for the hidden picture to speak to him. How that would happen—exactly what medium of communication the framed photo might avail itself of—he wasn't sure, but he knew he would recognize it when it came. The seconds ticked by. The print hung there incommunicado. Woody moved on to the next draped frame and waited. And the next. It wasn't until the seventh frame that he felt the hairs on the back of his neck stand up. Woody walked back to his table, set his drink down, smoothed a bar napkin, and took a sterling silver Cross pen from the inside breast pocket of his sport coat. On the napkin, he wrote "SOLD." He crossed back to the seventh frame and carefully, so as not to disturb the black drape, he tucked the top edge of the napkin behind the top edge of the frame so that the homemade sign hung down and rested lightly atop the black fabric. One of the dark-haired women at the bar split off from the group and glided up behind him.

"Did you peek?" the woman asked.

Woody felt the hairs on the back of his neck—he was sure they were the exact same hairs—rise again. "No," he answered without turning to look at the woman.

The woman's voice had a base coat of Southern charm that bled through the layers of Ivy League education and New York discourse. "How do you know you can afford it?"

Woody turned finally and looked directly into her eyes. "I'm sure we'll arrive at a fair price," he smiled.

"What if I tell you that the piece in question is five thousand dollars?"

"What if I offer you my 1959 Whitey Ford baseball card?"

"I don't know who Whitey Ford is."

"I don't know who *you* are."

Chapter 3

Jock Dejohnette had been born with a swollen and inflamed ego and six fingers on his left hand. He lost the sixth finger in a band saw accident in junior high school shop class. In doing so, he became the cautionary tale that Mr. Withers the shop teacher used to frighten an entire generation of pubescent would-be wood-workers. Nobody except Jock Dejohnette knew it had not been an accident.

Jock—he used the French pronunciation, Zhock—loved the fact that in New York one could dress all in black and not only avoid unwanted attention, but actually be fashionably normal. Try walking down the street at night, dressed all in black, in West Columbia, South Carolina or Butte, Montana. You might as well go to the local costume shop and ask for the Suspicious Person outfit. Jock stood in the recessed doorway of a closed tire shop on a corner in Brooklyn—the side door that faced 11th Street, as opposed to the front door on 4th Avenue. The alcove afforded him shadow and cover, effectively hiding him from the inattentive passer-by, yet passing as a casual hanging-out spot to anyone who might take the time to actually notice him. Across from him, an alleyway behind a building ended at a short fence. On the other side of that fence was the back yard of an unoccupied house that was under renovation. The house fronted 10th Street, and a short block away, back out on 4th Avenue, was the 9th Street subway station. Jock had chosen the location carefully. He carried a black cloth bag upon which "I ♥ NY" was emblazoned in red and white. The bag appeared to be well worn— tattered, even, in places. It probably would never occur to the casual observer that if one turned the bag inside-out and placed it over one's head, the ragged holes would align themselves perfectly with the wearer's eyes.

Jock Dejohnette heard the car coming up 11th Street long before he saw it. Not the car, actually. The car's stereo. The whoomp and thump of the bass competing with the screaming of the angry, obscene lyrics—a sound synergism whereby the abrasive whole exceeded the sum of its annoying parts. In a moment, a silver BMW slid slowly by Jock's lair. The windows were down. The young Latino man behind the wheel braked the rolling sound-quake to a halt at the red light. He was alone in the car. The car was alone on the street.

Jock moved swiftly from the alcove to the car's blind spot at the right rear of the BMW. The young man behind the wheel was too busy shouting along with the noise that spewed from the car's stereo to notice the figure all in black. In the few steps it had taken him to reach the car, Jock had flipped the black cloth bag inside out and slipped it over his head. In a carefully choreographed move, he stepped up, his right hand pulled the passenger door open, and his left hand jerked the gun from the waistband of his trousers. Before the startled driver could react, Jock was sitting beside him in the passenger seat, the muzzle of the gun pressed to the young man's head. Reaching over with his right hand, Jock turned off the ignition. A sudden silence filled the car.

"There. Isn't that better?" Jock's voice was menacingly calm from within the black hood.

"What the fuck you want?" The timbre of young man's voice was a grated mixture of fear and anger and surprise.

"First, I want absolute quiet. No shit from the stereo. No shit from you. No gunshots, if at all possible. Do you understand? Don't answer; just nod."

The young man nodded.

"Good. I'll shoot you if I have to, but if you do what I say, you'll walk away from here. Got it?"

"Yeah, but—" the young man started to answer.

"Don't talk," Jock interrupted. "Just nod."

The youth nodded.

"Now what this is...is what's called an object lesson. Do you have any idea how disrespectful and inconsiderate and annoying it is to other people when you ride around blasting that garbage from your stereo into the ears of people who don't want to listen to such trash? Don't answer. Of course you don't. Or rather didn't. After this, you will. Is this your car? Don't answer; just nod."

Another nod.

19

"Nice ride. You have insurance on it? Just nod."

A nod.

"Good. Do you know why I don't want to shoot you if I can help it? No, of course you don't. I don't want to shoot you if I can help it because I want you to deliver a message for me. A message to all of your friends. I want you to tell them what can happen to them if they're disrespectful and inconsiderate and annoying. Do you think you can deliver that message? Nod."

Nod.

"Excellent." Jock slipped a bottle of Hennessy's from his right jacket pocket. Holding the bottle between his knees, he opened it, then reached over and splashed the cognac all over the front of the young man. The young man gasped and pressed himself back against his seat. Jock poured the rest of the bottle into the floorboard on the passenger side, then he sat the bottle down on its side on the soaked floor mat. "Do you have any idea how flammable this stuff is?" he asked. "No, of course you don't." Jock lowered the gun so that it pointed at the young man's side. "Do you know that if I pulled the trigger now, not only would you have to contend with the bullet, but the muzzle blast would set you on fire? Burning to death's a bad way to go. But don't worry—do what I say, and you won't have to find out about burning to death. Take out your cell phone and put it on the dash. Just use your fingertips." The young man gingerly unclipped the cell phone from his side and set it on the car's dashboard. "Very nice. Now just be patient for one more minute." Jock reached and removed the keys from the car's ignition. "Sit very still now," he said, and he got out of the car. He walked behind the car and up along the driver's side. "Now step out very slowly and sit down on the pavement." The young Latino opened his car door, slipped out, and immediately sat down on the asphalt beside the car. "You know, this is going to make a great story to tell your friends. And I think you'll make them believe it. You know who's *not* going to believe it? The cops and your insurance company." Jock reached into his pocket and removed a cigarette and a disposable lighter. "Here," he said, and he handed them both to the young man. "You look like you could use a cigarette. Light it, but be careful not to set yourself on fire." The youth lit the cigarette and took a drag. Pointing the gun with his left hand, Jock extended his right hand toward the young man. "My lighter, I believe." The young man handed the lighter back and took another drag on the cigarette. "That should be enough," Jock reached down and took the cigarette from between the young man's lips. "It's hazardous to your health, you know." Jock opened the driver's side door, inserted the key in the ignition, and started the car. Immediately, the stereo boomed back to life. He reached into his jacket pocket and withdrew a small baggie of marijuana and slipped it between the car's console and the driver's seat. He picked up a small piece of paper, a

21

receipt, from the driver's side floor, lighted it with the disposable lighter, and dropped it into the floorboard of the passenger side of the car. The blaze whooshed to life. Jock flipped the cigarette into the inferno, shut the driver's side door, and turned to the young man. He pointed down 11th Street in the direction from which the young man had come. "I'd run about a block down that way if I were you," he said. The young man crawled a short distance on his hands and feet before he rose and began to run. Jock slipped the gun into the waistband of his pants, turned and slipped into the alley. As he got to the short fence, Jock pulled the hood from his head. He hopped the fence, and by the time he was coming out onto 10th Street, he had turned the hood back into the innocuous black bag and moved the gun from his waistband to the bag. The sounds from the car's stereo skipped, then squealed, then fell quiet as the flames engulfed the dashboard of the silver BMW. Jock rounded the corner at 4th Avenue and stepped into the subway station. He stopped and picked up a discarded *Voice*, stuffed it into his bag and headed for the turnstile.

Chapter 4

When Casey called his mom to say he was coming to visit, Katie Frye was trimming the small plot of grass that passed for a backyard—a wrought-iron fenced putting-green surface surrounded by rose bushes, daffodils, and flowering ivy that climbed the fence in a lush green swarm. She clipped the grass by hand, using a pair of stainless steel Fisgar scissors. It was more like grooming a pet than yard work, but she liked to get personal with the things she raised in the black dirt she'd had trucked in and dumped and spread at the rear of her gallery in an old building in downtown Norfolk. When she asked what was wrong, he'd said "nothing," but it was there in his voice. She could hear trouble—and maybe a touch of scared—ducking and hiding among her son's laughs and quips. And when she knew trouble was coming to visit, she liked to get her hands dirty—to feel the sun-warmed black earth in her hands and to pet and groom the green growing things that she'd coaxed from that earth.

Chapter 5

She pronounced it *Mer*ilee—as in "Merrily we roll along"—as opposed to Meri*lee*. The second time Woody and Merilee made love—correction—on the second *occasion* of their lovemaking—the second *time* was during the first *occasion*, as was the third time—an opening-new-presents-on-Christmas-morning kind of excitement coursing through them in their hormonal hunger for the caress and press of new naked flesh—but on the second *occasion*, they discovered the buzz. It was during a slow moment—in the relaxed dreaminess after lovemaking—the first time on the second occasion. They had teased each other before and during the sex—coupled and moved with an excruciatingly thrilling slowness—savoring each smooth push and pull until the sensations made their breaths catch and come in shallow gasps while they froze and teetered on the brink of dissolving in the liquid explosion that one more push would produce. The lights were on in the room, as they had been on the first occasion, so that they could see each other and see each other seeing each other. Woody had looked down to see where they were joined.

"You're watching us fuck," Merilee had whispered. He wasn't sure what to say, how to respond. "Don't you love the way it looks—the way we fit together?" she asked.

"Yes," Woody hissed.

"Me, too," she said, her breaths were short

and shallow. "Watch," she spoke softly, as she rolled her hips ever-so slightly.

That did it. They both watched as he pushed in one more time, and then they surrendered to the sparkly liquid rush that washed over them and swept them both away.

Afterwards they lay side by side, languishing in the tingle of exquisitely touchous nerve endings and allowed their breathing to return to normal. After a couple of minutes, Merilee spoke.

"Did I shock you—the words I used? Did it bother you?"

"Jesus, no—" he said, "—I loved it."

Woody rolled onto his left side, facing her, and reached out to lightly brush the back side of his right hand along her ribcage and over the gentle swell of her tummy. And that's when they buzzed.

It was a buzz you could feel and, if you listened very carefully, you could hear. Woody began almost immediately to try to puzzle out the forces at work. There were whiffs and swirls, dollops and dashes of electro-magnetism, static electricity, bio-chemistry, Memphis soulmate stew, midnight mojo, and at least eleven secret herbs and spices known only to Cupid's personal chef. The sensation was one of running your hand lightly over the bristle tips of an electric cotton candy hairbrush—of petting a neon kitten. What secret marriage of bio-recipe and cosmic circuitry was at work here? What mystic Rumpelstiltskin could spin the low voltage silk from which these force-field

25

play-clothes were tailored? His mind got a running start to jump the fence surrounding the playground of possibilities, but Merilee's voice broke his stride.

"We buzzed," she whispered.

"I know," he answered. "Did you ever buzz before?"

"No," she smiled. "Turn out the lights."

He got up, snapped off the lights, and climbed back into bed beside her. As they reached for each other, not quite touching, the buzz-meister upped the ante. It saw their tingle and raised them a light show. Under the cover of darkness, the buzz slipped into its aura pajamas.

"We glow, too," Marilee's voice was tinged more with curiosity than surprise.

"Yep. Glow and buzz. Buzz and glow," Woody tagged on. "You know what this means, don't you?"

"Hmmmm," she buzzed. "I don't think so. What does it mean?"

"Damn," he glowed. "I was hoping you knew." He sighed. "Something very good, I suspect. Or..." and he paused, "...something very strangely bad."

"I vote for something very good," Merilee raised her eyebrows.

"Hold that thought," Woody said, as his fingertips resumed playing buzzy games with the smooth contours of her new lightning bug birthday suit.

Chapter 6

On the check-out counter near the cash register in a small convenience store in Norfolk, someone had set up a sheet of heavy cardboard. It had a triangle of cardboard taped to the back to form a pedestal leg like on the back of a picture frame, so that it would stand up. The front was covered with a piece of slick, dark blue paper, glued down, with slots cut into it so that coins could be fitted into the slots. At the top of the paper was a picture of a young boy—four, maybe five years old—and a typed note that read: "Jeremy Jernigan needs a kidney transplant. Until one becomes available, your change can help pay for his dialysis. Please help." The sheet was about half filled with coins, mostly quarters, stuck halfway into the slots. Casey Frye thought of that homemade cardboard charity card as he looked up at the blue-black sky with its huge half moon stuck there like the only coin donated to a very needy world. He knew there would be no Save-Casey-Frye's-Balls drive. His mom would be as supportive as she could be—emotionally, morally, and with what she could muster financially—but she didn't—*couldn't*, actually, he thought—understand the full impact of what the doctors were advocating. To her it was as simple as lose-your-balls, save-your-life—they were only balls. Only balls. He thought of going through life as No-Balls Frye. And he thought of Debbie. His fiancée. His next stop. This was not a conversation he was looking forward to. *Better do it now*, he thought, *while I've still got the balls for it.*

Chapter 7

Buddha-dharma reminds us (it doesn't *teach* us because this is something we already know) that not only is everything subject to change, but that everything *does* change. And every*one*. Once Woody accepted the fact that he was not who he once was, nor would he ever be who he is now, he saw that there was no reason to cling to the false notion of an identity that he had built for himself and for others. Except he wasn't Woody Zildjian when he took the cosmic reminder to heart and took it at its word. He was Leonard Lupo. Leonardo, actually. Leonardo L. Lupo. But, more commonly...Lennie. Lennie-of-Long-Ago.

Lennie sat at the bar and glanced up at the Eleven O'Clock News. Marvin Gaye had been shot dead in a motel room by his father. Lennie wondered briefly how someone lived with himself after he'd killed his own son.

It was the last week he had been Lennie Lupo—the week before he became Ray Black.

"Did you make a list?" Lennie began as soon as the man arrived.

"... List?" the man repeated as he sat down.

"Like I suggested. A list of any possible complications."

"Oh. Yeah."

"And?"

"Very short list."

29

"Like what?"

"Beth."

"Beth Black? Your ex?"

"Yeah."

"And exactly what is the complication?"

"It's an emotional complication."

"Who's on the hook?"

"Hook?"

"You said an emotional complication. That means—to me, at least—that somebody's still on the hook. Either you've got the hook still in your lip, and she's holding the line, or vice versa. Which is it?"

"It may be a little of both."

"Both? You both still have each other on the line? What the hell is that? So why aren't you still together?"

"It's complicated."

"Which is why it made it to the short list of complications. I get that part. Now what I need to understand is the exact nature of the complication. If I might have to deal with the complication, I need to know as much about it as possible. Right?"

"Right."

"So why aren't the two of you still together?"

"Because I fucked up."

"You told me that. That was the reason for the divorce. That I understand. What I don't understand is why there's still a complication. Are you telling me you still love her?"

"Yeah. I suppose so."

"There's no supposing, Don. I need to know. If I'm going to *be* Don Black, I need all the Don Black info there is. All of it. Including all the shit in the little hidden compartments. Got it?"

"Yeah."

"So do you still love her?"

"Yeah."

"What about her? You said both of you were still hooked. You think she still loves you?"

"I think so. I'm pretty sure. Yeah."

Sigh. "Any chance of getting back together? Any chance at all?"

"No."

"You're absolutely sure?"

"I'm sure."

"Tell me. We can't sit here and play Twenty Questions about this. I need it all. Tell me the whole thing, so I can try to get a take on how sure 'sure' is."

"She's getting re-married. Moving to San Francisco."

"If the two of you are still tugging on each other's line, why is she marrying someone else?"

"I fucked up again."

"The getting married thing and the moving—she's not going to back out?"

"No."

"How do you know?"

"I know her."

"You're not going to get all crazy and go

31

chasing after her out in California?"

"No. I can't."

"That's right. You can't. Not if we do this."

"I know."

"What about her? She's not going to get out there and change her mind?"

"No way."

"Not even if this guy turns out to be a complete asshole?"

"No."

"Not even if he turns out to be some wacko who starts beating her up or something?"

"She wouldn't put up with that. She'd leave him."

"Exactly. But how do you know she wouldn't come looking for you then?"

"She just wouldn't."

"It wouldn't do at all, you know, for her to come looking for you two years down the road and find me."

"It won't happen."

"So tell me why. Convince me."

"She's finally come into her own. Found herself. Become her own person. She wouldn't do anything to jeopardize that. As much as we care for each other, I think she believes I'm somehow a threat to that independence."

"And this new guy she's marrying. He's not?"

"He's marrying the new Beth. With me, I think she's afraid there might be a relapse."

32

"And your happiness—for lack of a better term—you can just let this happen?"

"It's not up to me. It's happening. Happened. As for my happiness—if my cup was running over, so to speak, I'd stay just who I am. Right?"

"Right."

"I really want her to do what's best for her."

"Sounds pretty rehearsed."

"Maybe it does. I don't know. But I really mean it."

"I know you said you fucked up—the thing with the blonde—but why didn't you and Beth work that out?"

"It was too big to work out. Too big a betrayal."

"She never betrayed you?"

"What do you mean?"

"She never fucked up?"

"Yeah. Once. That I know of."

"And?"

"We worked it out."

"You mean *you* worked it out. You worked out her fuck-up, but she wouldn't work out yours."

"No. *I* wouldn't work out mine."

"Ah."

"When she told me about her having an affair—I don't know—yeah, I was hurt—I thought at the time there couldn't possibly be any worse hurt. Turns out I was wrong about that, too. But, as hurt as I was—as angry as I was—as much as I wanted to scream at her, to call her a stupid cunt, and storm out of the house and go get drunk—I was more afraid for her. For what telling me about it was doing to her. For how bad *she* was hurting. Sounds crazy, huh?"

"The best kind of love is always a little crazy.

"I guess."

"So you had your affair to get even?"

"No. I don't think so. At least not consciously. I don't know—maybe that was somewhere in the mix."

"And when you told her?"

"It was different."

"How was it different?"

"When she told me, her affair was in the past. It was over. Done. The way she told me, there was almost this unspoken 'now what?' quality about it. When I told her, I was basically telling her on my way out the door. I was leaving."

"Why?"

"I thought then that it was to go to the other woman. But what it was was I couldn't live with it, so in my mind I guess I was thinking, 'So then why should *she*?' Why should either of us have to live with it?"

"I'm thinking maybe you still can't live with it."

"I don't know."

"It's okay. I can live with it. ... Okay—here's what I want you to do. Give the whole thing twenty-four hours more thought. I'll do the same thing. We'll meet back here Sunday and decide to do it or dump it. Okay?"

"Okay."

"No other complications, right? You're sure?"

"I'm sure." He paused, almost like he didn't want to ask. "What about you?"

"What about me?"

"Any...complications?"

"My life got uncomplicated *for* me." He took a drink and crunched a piece of ice with his teeth. "A drunk driver wiped the slate clean. All that I was. And all that I was planning on being. ... Drink up." Lennie lit a cigarette and offered one to the man he was considering becoming.

"I don't smoke."

"Could be you're getting ready to start in a few days. Just one of the things for you to consider while there is time."

"While there is time..." Will there be a time when there is no more time? That hardly seems likely, or even possible. Because a *time* in which there is no time would still be a *time*. Just as there can be no vacuum in which there is no nothing, there can be no time in which there is no time. A vacuum without absolutely nothing is not a vacuum, so a vacuum in which there is another vacuum is filled with something. You cannot have a vacuum filled with a vacuum because the presence of the minor vacuum within the major vacuum negates the vacuity of the major vacuum. Once the sands of time cease to flow through the hourglass, they do not cease to be sands; they only cease to be flowing sands. For the moment. A still moment, but a moment nonetheless. We could go on and on with this if there were time. "If there were time..." Ah. But as we've just seen, there must *be* time. Thus the hourglass up-ends itself, restores the flow to the sands, and, basically, brings us back to where we were before we began this tip-toe down the primrose cul-de-sac. And having arrived back where we began, we look down a different path of time.

Chapter 8

As Woody Zildjian slept, he was surprised to find himself sitting behind the wheel of his father's 1962 Chevy BelAir. He was parked on the shoulder of a strange, dark road, the car's engine running. The flash of the bubble gum machine light atop a police car parked behind him washed through the interior of his car with a steady red pulse—a broad red beam that he could somehow physically feel on the back of his neck each time it swept through the car. With each flash, he could see his face reflected in the rear view mirror. Through it was the same face he had seen in the mirror that same morning—red-tinted, but still, his here-and-now face—he knew he was only sixteen years old as he sat there in the cavernous interior of the BelAir. Just outside the open window of the driver's door, he could see the Sam Browne-girded shape of a large cop—the officer's head lost in the darkness above the window. He passed his driver's license through the open window into the waiting hand of the faceless lawman.

"Nice try," an official voice spoke from the darkness, "but this isn't you."

"Oh," he answered, "wait, wait," and he fumbled through his wallet and pulled out another driver's license. He handed the license through the window.

"Nice try," the voice repeated, "but this isn't

you."

"I know, I know," he heard the panic in his own voice. "It's right here; I've got it right here." He produced another card from his wallet and offered it to the hand that reached through the window.

"Nice try," the voice didn't miss a beat, "but this isn't you."

"I've got it here somewhere," he pleaded. "Honest, I know it's here somewhere." But as he tried to pull yet another DL from his wallet, it stretched like melted plastic, separating into drooping elastic shreds that stuck to his fingers and the big BelAir steering wheel.

The cop began to laugh—a wicked, sneering laugh that reverberated in time to the sweep of the red flashing light.

He threw the car into gear and stomped the accelerator. Gravel flew. He felt the tires catch the pavement; the rubber squealed. The wind rushed through the open window as he raced along the black ribbon of the road, but somehow the officer remained at the window, as if standing on a shelf just outside the car door. The red light kept up its steady red sweep. The laugh grew louder, filled the car. He fumbled with the volume control knob of the car radio, as if he could turn down the booming laughter.

He felt the rear end of the Chevy begin to swerve and to come around. He fought the wheel for control, but the car began to spin into the darkness and the laughter. He felt himself pitch forward through where the windshield should have been, and he bolted upright, awake in the darkness of the bedroom.

"Fuck!" he muttered, then sank back into the warm confines of his new bed.

Casey Frye sat up in his bed and scrubbed the palms of his hands up and down over his eyes, as he disengaged himself from his dream. He didn't really understand it, but it was, after all, only a dream and dreams often made no sense. In the dream, he had found himself dressed in a highway patrolman's uniform, standing beside a stopped car—an old car. Someone—someone whose face was lost in the shadow of the car's interior kept handing him different driver's licenses, and for some reason he found each one funnier than the last. As the car sped off, he found himself surfing a current of air alongside the speeding car, and that was the funniest thing of all. He awoke to the sound of his own laughter.

"Fuck!" he said and rubbed his eyes again with the heels of his palms, then he fell back into the cushiony lap of his pillow.

Chapter 9

Debbie Dockery loved kids. She already had names picked out for the two children that she knew in the maternal cockles of her heart that she and Casey were going to have—Wally and Anastasia—a boy and a girl. Wally after her father, Walter Dockery—and also because she had harbored a crush on Wally Cleaver, Beaver's older brother, from re-runs since she was a little girl. Anastasia because she just thought it was such a "precious sounding" name, and because it was so little used lately, and because it had an element of the mysterious and regal about it. She thought that, at times, they might call her Annie when she was being especially cute or especially exasperating in a cute way, but by and large, it would be Anastasia proper. It was, in fact, her answer to Casey's marriage proposal. When he finally asked her the question, "Will you marry me?" her eyes got wide, then welled up with tears of happiness, and she replied, "Oh, my God, Casey—can we have two children—a boy and a girl—and name them Wally and Anastasia? Can we?" Of all the response scenarios that Casey had played out in his head, this one was a surprise.

"Does that mean 'yes'?" he asked.

"Yes, yes, yes," she said, "Can we?"

"Sure," Casey said. And so, it was part of the plan from the beginning.

As soon as Casey had told her what the

doctor had said, she had begun to cry. Casey couldn't help but wonder for a moment whether the tears were for him or for Wally and Anastasia.

And then she had said, "It doesn't matter, Casey. We're not giving up. But even if worse comes to worse, it doesn't matter. I love you."

Of all the response scenarios he had played out in his head, this was better than he thought he could have hoped for. He especially liked the "we" in the "not giving up" part. She had a vested dream interest in those balls, too.

Chapter 10

The deal between Lennie Lupo and Don Black had started a few weeks earlier—a Friday night in a bar in Atlanta, nearly one o'clock in the morning, Eastern Hourglass Time. They had been sitting side-by-side at the bar for a while. Don sat on a stool directly to the right of the waitress' station at the bar. Lennie sat on the stool to his right. Lennie took a sip of his rum and Coke, used the little plastic stir-stick to jab at the slice of lime floating among the few remaining ice cubes, then he fished a cigarette from the pack in his jacket pocket, planted it in the corner of his mouth, and fired it up. When he blew out the first jet of smoke, it happened to be in the direction where Don was sitting. Don coughed an irritated little cough—more a sound of displeasure than of actual expectoration—and waved the smoke away with his hand.

"Sorry," Lennie offered. It was more an exercise in polite discourse than actual heart-felt contrition. But he did offer it.

Don glanced his way, turned his nose up slightly, and said something breathy and disapproving that sounded like "shoo." Lennie's eyes narrowed, his upper lip curled, and his reply resonated in the lower chambers of his throat, "Grrrrrrrrrrr."

Don whipped his head back around, looking away from the suddenly high-strange character who sat beside him. Now, though, he found himself looking at the waitress who had walked up to the wait station. The grin on her face combined with something she did with her eyebrows to say that she was laughing not with him, but *at* him. The look all but asked him if he'd like a shot of testosterone to go with that beer. He patted his breast pockets and let his hands slide down his belly, as if frisking himself for a trace of male pride. Then he turned back to Lennie, who had returned his attention to harpooning citrus. Dressed all in black—black jeans, black tee shirt, what appeared to be a black silk sportcoat—the stranger—now that he wasn't growling—looked as if his wardrobe was more menacing than his face, which appeared remarkably calm now. It was an odd—puzzling if you actually took the time to think about it—mix. Something about the stranger reminded Don of the gentleman gunslinger or gambler of old TV westerns. One of the Mavericks, maybe. Bret? Bart? He didn't have time to sort them out right then.

"Did you *growl* at me?" Don asked. Somewhere between his intention and his delivery, though, the question lost all sense of bravado and came across more quizzical than challenging.

Lennie turned and looked at him, but didn't say anything—just looked him in the eye. The look was impassive. Not threatening or confrontational, really. A blank stare. A look that offered no answer—one that didn't invite further communication, but it did seem to await it. After what seemed an inordinately long silence, Don

43

offered, "I've never been growled at."

"I'm guessing you have," Lennie finally spoke. "You've just never been growled at to your face."

"I didn't mean anything—about your smoking, I mean. It just went in my face, is all."

"People come to bars to smoke. And to drink. And to pretend they're gonna get lucky with the waitress." Lennie said the last part loud enough for the waitress to hear. She pretended not to hear, but her smile gave her away. "'Course they never really do. One in a million, maybe. Fewer than that, probably. About the same odds as winning the lottery." Don glanced back at the waitress. She rolled her eyes and walked away. "Not your lucky day, I guess," Lennie tagged.

"Not my lucky year," Don shook his head. "Not my lucky decade."

"Luck changes," Lennie noted, then took a drink of his rum and coke.

Don offered his hand. "Don," he said, "Don Black."

"I already did," Lennie answered.

"Huh?"

"Nevermind," Lennie shook his head slightly. He took Don's hand, tense with the effort to make a firm showing of itself, yet still only half succeeding. "Lennie Lupo."

"Hey—" the handshake over, Don withdrew his hand, "—great name."

"I didn't pick it," Lennie deadpanned.

"Guess not," Don nodded.

"But I did choose to keep it," Lennie added.

"Huh?" Clearly, Don didn't get the implication.

"You don't like your name—change it. You don't like your life—change it," Lennie plucked the short cigarette stub from the ashtray and took a drag that took a quick hot bite of his lip.

"Just like that, huh?" Don raised his eyebrows.

Lennie crushed out the butt. "Just like that."

They were quiet for a moment. Don took a swig of beer. Lennie put his glass to his lips and let the cool liquid bathe the spot on his lip that the cigarette had nipped.

"Oh! I get it," Don suddenly turned back to Lennie. His right hand waved up and down in front of Lennie as if granting him absolution. "Don black. Like dress all in black, right?" Don smiled and nodded again. "You're quick. The way you just came right back with that. What're you—like, a comedy writer or something?"

"No," Lennie resisted the impulse to roll his eyes.

"So what do you do then?" Don persisted.

Lennie took a deep breath and released it. "I own a bar," he said.

"Yeah?" Don perked up, "Oh, wait. Here? You own *this* bar?"

"Not here." Lennie finished his drink and raised his glass to the bartender in the international sign for "another one, just like the other one."

"Where?" his neighbor pressed on.

"Key West," he said. The bartender began making a fresh drink, so he sat his empty glass on the inside edge of the bar.

"Oh, wow! Key West! That's got to be fantastic, man!"

"Fantastic barely covers it," Lennie said flatly.

The waitress came back. She cast Lennie a look. It was a look he recognized. It was full of if-only-I-weren'ts. "If only I weren't working." "If only I weren't married." "If only I weren't surrounded by my friends with whom you would simply never fit in." It was a look that sometimes yielded a telephone number scribbled on a folded slip of paper and discreetly slipped into his hand by a woman as she slid by on her way to the powder room.

Lennie never understood exactly what women saw in him. He knew he was not unattractive—his was a face, if not *GQ* handsome, then with character. It was, however, a face that women trusted for some reason—that they wanted to tell things to. He just wasn't sure why. And trust, he had discovered, was the secret ingredient in sex.

The realization had come to him one night several years ago after he watched a woman named Lara send her blind date away into the moist Key West night. She was a semi-regular at the bar, but not a bar-fly by any stretch of the imagination. She was just a young working woman looking—as so many were—for Mr. Right, and, instead, constantly encountering Mr. As-Right-As-You-Need-Me-To-Be-Until-I-Get-What-I-Want.

She seemed to have chosen Lupo's as the after-dinner spot to bring the blind dates that family and friends and, most recently, a dating service had conjured up as pretenders to the Mr. Right crown. Lupo's Bar provided just the right mix of privacy and lighting and alcohol to bring out the true colors of the pretenders, and just the right mix of public and people-who-know-me to send them away with very little chance of a scene.

After she walked the latest loser to the door, Lara came back to the bar and stared for a moment at the trustworthy face of Lennie Lupo at the end of the bar. She picked up her drink, her purse, and her expectations for the evening, and relocated to the barstool beside Lennie.

Lennie resorted to quoting Buffett. "Tried and I tried, but I don't understand. Never seems to work out the way I had it planned."

Lara laughed. "Maybe I've just set the bar too high," she said.

"A high bar's not such a bad thing, really," Lennie answered. "Of course that depends on whether you're expecting people to pole vault or limbo."

"Ah," she nodded, "that perspective thing. Well, if they can't even figure out the game, how can they ever expect to win?"

47

"There's a line in there somewhere about whether you're looking for somebody with a pole or somebody prepared to go down, but I'm just not clever enough to come up with it."

"I suspect you're more clever than you let on," she smiled.

"I'll tell you how not-clever I am. I'm not even sure if it's 'more clever' or 'cleverer'," Lennie smiled back and took a sip of his drink.

"I like to have a good time, too," she said. "But if they can't be honest sitting here at the bar, what the hell can I expect in bed?" She paused. "Does that shock you?"

Lennie puzzled briefly about why women asked him so often if they shocked him. He knew he hadn't registered anything close to shock, and he didn't think he just had the look of someone who was easily shockable. *Maybe they're* trying *to shock me*, he thought. Then he wondered why. What did women think there was to gain by shocking him?

"Sorry, but I mean, I like sex as much as anyone," she continued. Maybe she took his moment of puzzlement as affirmation that he was, in fact, shocked. "I guess you've seen me—meeting these guys and all. I don't think I'm asking too much that they just be honest with me. I mean, is that asking too much?"

"I don't think so," he tossed in.

"I mean, for God's sake, I was seeing a married man for nearly six months. My mother would have a stroke, but at least he was honest about it. He told me up front he was married. I knew what I was getting into. I don't think that makes me a bad person, does it?"

"I don't think so," Lennie offered.

"Thank you. Me, neither. He was very up front with me. It was just sex. It was entirely my decision."

Briefly, Lennie felt philosophically inadequate. "Well, you don't have to justify any—" he started to say.

"I'm not saying I'm proud of it," she interrupted, "I'm just saying it was honest, is all. Everything was up front."

"Honest is good," was all he could come up with.

"But you want to know the sad thing?" she continued.

"Well, I imagine there are *lots* of—" he started to insert.

She interrupted again, "It never, you know, 'worked' for me. You know what I mean?"

"'Worked' for you? I'm not sure—" but he was cut off again.

"Worked for me," she forged ahead. "You know. I never had, you know, an orgasm. The whole time."

"Oh," Lennie nodded. It was time to light a cigarette. And so he did.

"I mean, it's sad, but it's not really all that unusual, I don't think. Do you? Because, I mean, I've never, you know, done that."

49

That did pique his interest. "Never?"

"Not with anyone else. I mean, I don't want to go into that, but I do know what it feels like, but just not with someone else. If you know what I mean."

"I think I do," he said. Lennie felt suddenly and strangely professorial, in a therapist sort of way. "Well, it's a trust thing," he proffered.

"Exactly!" she nodded vigorously, "and, I mean, how do you know who to trust? And it's not like they're not trying—to make me feel good, I mean—some of them, anyway. I mean, they try to wait, or they try things with—you know, oral things and all—but, I don't know—sometimes it's just easier to fake it. So they won't feel bad, you know. But it just doesn't work. For me, anyway. I don't know what the problem is."

And that's when it occurred to him. That's when Lennie discovered the line that rang true for them. For the women.

"You know what I've discovered that most women want?" he smiled knowingly. "They want someone to hold them while it happens."

"Hold them?" She was genuinely interested.

"Yeah," Lennie proposed, "just hold them. It's not all this thrusting and pounding, or any kind of magic tongue technique. It's just a matter of a patient hand on just the right spot and holding her so that she knows that it's okay—okay to just let it happen."

Aristotle would have been proud. It was a

moment of clarity—a moment of pure learning and self-discovery, arrived at through the open exchange of ideas—one question prompting another—honest comment giving rise to honest comment—an intellectual journey to the precise, slippery, pink core of absolute truth.

Later, as the ocean had its way with the beach beyond Lennie's house, the two of them put their new-found knowledge to the test. They both passed with screaming colors.

Chapter 11

In 1906, a French physician, Alexis Carrel, in Chicago, transplanted a heart into a dog and a kidney into a cat. Neither Fido nor Fluffy survived. That same year, two transplant attempts were made by Mathieu Jaboulay: the first, a pig's kidney into a woman; the second, a goat's liver into another woman. Neither woman fared any better than Fido and Fluffy. In 1954, Dr. Joseph E. Murray performed the first *successful* organ transplant—a kidney—in Boston. He received the Nobel Prize. In 1968, the first successful heart transplant was performed by Dr. Norman Shumway in Stanford, California.

No one really knows when we started cutting off men's testicles. Certainly, it predates the surgical procedure known as an orchiectomy. Ancient Rome, Persia, the Byzantine and the Ottoman empires, societies in both Africa and Asia, all had their eunuchs. In the Bible, in Matthew 19:12, Jesus even comments on "eunuchs...made...eunuchs for the kingdom of heaven's sake." "Well, for heaven's sake!" Augustine supposedly pointed out, "He was just making an allegorical reference to priestly celibacy." We do have a pretty good idea that the first vasectomy was the work of Dr. Harry C. Sharp, in 1899, at the Jefferson Reformatory in Indiana. It was a treatment to "cure" a "criminal"—a compulsive masturbator. It worked so well on the young delinquent that Dr. Sharp went ahead and "cured" forty-one other youthful criminal chicken-chokers. Well, for heaven's sake!—there's a little cautionary tale for sex ed class. The first reversal of a vasectomy was in 1919 by W.C. Quinby. One has to wonder if the patient had ever done time in Indiana.

Dr. Mark Strejc of Tidewater Urological Associates in Norfolk, Virginia really, really, reeeaaalllly wanted a "first successful" something after his M.D. credentials. It had occurred to Dr. Strejc that a testicular transplant was little more than a vasectomy reversal, when you came right down to it. Microsurgical reattachment of the vans deferens, restoration of the blood supply, and—zip!—done and done. The hardest part would be finding a suitable donor—preferably a blood relative who was receptive to the argument that, like kidneys, you've got two of them and one is all you really need. But then again, though many a man has scratched his balls—sometimes at entirely inappropriate times or places—it's hardly ever because he's itching to give one away.

Dr. Strejc had a golfing buddy. Walter Dockery. And Walter Dockery's future son-in-law, the *pater designatus* of Wally and Anastasia, had a problem. It was the kind of problem that made Dr. Strejc say, "Hmmmmmm."

Chapter 12

Don Black sat and thought of the decline of his station in life—decline, as he perceived it. Though it might be argued fairly convincingly that he had never been truly happy with his life, he had enjoyed the facade of prestige that accompanied the title of vice-president at the Merchants' and Farmers' Bank of Haversham. The position afforded him the kind of power that sets certain individuals apart from the average people in small towns. The characteristic that defines "average" people is powerlessness. The trait is particularly dominant—almost genetic—in small towns because everybody knows everybody. Everybody knows the few individuals who have any kind of power and over whom they have it. The powerful-powerless caste system is entrenched to the point that any mobility—upward or downward—is so rare as to be the stuff of which local legends are made. As infrequent and notable as the instances of upward mobility are, the few falls from power are so dramatic that they achieve near Greek tragic proportions.

In the late-1960s, Rat Miller owned two drugstores and a supermarket. Prior to the arrival of Eckerd's, Miller's had been the only two drugstores in town. The Piggly Wiggly had been around long enough that it wasn't viewed so much as a competitor to Miller's Market as merely an alternative. Folks patronized both Miller's Market and the Piggly Wiggly without any feelings of having betrayed one or the other. The pharmacies were another story. One took one's prescriptions either to Miller's #1 or #2 *or* to Eckerd's. One was either in the Miller camp or the Eckerd's. It was a choice as clear as what church one attended.

In those days, Richard Miller—or Doc, as he was most often called, for those were the days before he became Rat Miller—split his work week behind the pharmacy counter evenly at Miller's #1 and Miller's #2. Mondays, Wednesdays, and Fridays, he was at #1. Tuesdays, Thursdays, and Saturdays, he spent at #2. Mr. Pollard, the other pharmacist, rotated at the exact opposite schedule. Doc Miller felt it was important that people saw him behind the counter at both locations. His nephew, Carl Carpenter—his late sister's son— managed the supermarket. Again, Doc Miller thought it was important that folks see a family presence. So there was Miller Drugs #1, Miller Drugs #2, and Miller's Market. And there was Dot—Doc's wife, to whom he was devoted.

Dot Miller did not work outside the home. Her domesticity was in keeping with her position in the community. Outside the home, she was appropriately active in the church and served on the board for the public library, until "the illness," as it was commonly referred to. "The illness" was a particularly aggressive uterine cancer. "The illness" had quietly established its metastic infrastructure before it announced its shattering presence in the

Millers' genteel life. And though Doc Miller brought the full resources of his years of pharmaceutical experience, as well as two drug stores' stocks of modern medicines to the fight, "the illness" would not be denied the claim it had staked on Doc's Dot. It took her on Good Friday, and when Easter passed with no miraculously risen Dot, something apparently happened in the mind of Doc Miller.

In the wee hours of Monday morning, Doc Miller padlocked and boarded up Miller Drugs #1, Miller Drugs #2, and Miller's Market. You can imagine the progression from confusion to fear to anger and disgust that played itself out among the employees and customers, the distributors, reps, and creditors, the loyal and the merely curious. In less than six months, the machineries of law and social judgment joined forces with a newly acquired taste for cheap liquor to reduce Doc Miller's holdings to the clothes on his back. It was shortly thereafter that Doc Miller took up residence beneath the old cotton warehouse on Depot Street and, in doing so, became Rat Miller. And a new legend took its place among Haversham's oral history.

Don Black knew his decline was more the stuff of small town small talk than the stuff that legends are made of. His family was of that ilk that one would call prominent in Haversham. Make that his *father's* family, for the family and all the assets that made it prominent were certainly his father's in the most proprietary sense. Americus Black was a

56

self-made man of the old school. Americus had met Aurelia Baccus at the U.S.O. Servicemen's Center in Charleston near the end of the war—World War II. Americus had done his time in the Atlantic, and in the course of that doing had sustained a combat injury—a severe burn to his left leg which wrapped his left knee in scar tissue so substantial that his left leg was never fully bendable again. Somehow, Americus took the injury and sauntered right past the "lame" image and slipped instead very comfortably and very permanently into "swashbuckling." It fit him to a "T." Aurelia had never been truly swashbuckled. She had come to Charleston with the hesitant permission of her father, George, a Greek immigrant who had established the Acropolis Cafe on Main Street in Haversham some sixteen years before. There is a phenomenon that borders on truism in small towns that even if you are born there, unless your family's roots in the community are as deep as the memories of the town's oldest citizens, you are never truly "from there." And yet, having been born there, Aurelia knew only the pleasant acceptance that comes from a kind of communal decision that someone—even though not really "from there" yet—was "on the right track." She may not have known the full embrace of being "from there," but neither had she ever felt truly "foreign." Her father George, though, knew the feeling all too well. His acceptance within the community was the conditional sort that resides within the boundaries of expressions like: "Well, ya know—he's a pretty good ol' boy—for a foreigner, I mean." When Haversham began to send its sons off to foreign lands, George saw his foreignness reflected in his customers' eyes. They still came into the cafe, and they still drank from his "bottomless coffee cup" and ordered their eggs and grits early and their egg salad sandwiches at lunch, but George had no sons to send. He displayed an American flag in front of the cafe and hung Victory Bond posters in the front window, but with each blue-starred—some later giving way to gold-starred—"Son in Service" flag that went up in a window in town, for reasons he couldn't put into words, George more and more felt something akin to guilt. It was for that reason that when his daughter came to him with a notion that he would have otherwise surely dismissed—a notion that she could help out in the war effort by serving doughnuts and coffee at the U.S.O. Servicemen's Center in Charleston—George took a deep breath and quietly nodded his assent, and the wheels were set in motion that delivered Aurelia into the swashbuckling path of Petty Officer Second Class Americus Black.

The marriage of Americus Black and Aurelia Baccus was more than the merging of two A.B.s—initials and blood types—clearly more than coincidence, as some of the more fate-minded people in town liked to point out; the couple became a genuine force within the community, a synergism that rose with surprising speed—

considering the "not from there" handicap—to big-fish-in-a-small-pond prominence. Shortly after the war, Americus established Haversham's first, and for a long time, *only* automobile dealership—AB Chevrolet. In spite of how hard George Baccus wished and prayed for a grandson, Americus and Aurelia's first issue was a daughter. They played with A and B naming possibilities and finally settled on Abbie. At age nine, Abbie did not surrender "only child" status graciously. When baby Donald (named after one of Americus' wartime buddies—a man Americus credited with saving his life, and who, in turn, credited Americus with saving his life, as well) was old enough to lie in his crib and take his own bottle without having to be held, Abbie would routinely sneak in and loosen the cap around the nipple so that the milk would leak all over young Donald and the bedclothes. His parents found the baby's ability to loosen the cap curious the first couple of times it happened; then, increasingly, they simply found it an annoying problem for which they blamed the infant. The practice would define Don's relationship with his sister for life.

AB Chevrolet became an institution in Haversham. The dealership sponsored little league teams and even donated a car once to be raffled off to raise money to expand and update the hospital emergency room. Americus Black became known for his generous contributions to worthy causes and organizations—all tax-deductible. "Good charity is part of good business," he liked to say. Don decided early that the car business was not for him—especially if it meant working for his father. As he made the connection between people "buying" cars from his father, but going to the bank for approval to actually make their purchases, Don decided that bankers were higher in the food chain than car salesmen. When he took off for the University of Georgia, Don already was playing a fantasy scenario in his head that involved his father calling him at the bank to ask—no, to beg—him to reconsider the interest rates and loan approval criteria that were cutting into AB Chevrolet's monthly sales quotas. As do most fantasies, the scenario never made it outside the confines of Donald's headache-prone noggin.

Don Black made his debut into the banking industry as a loan officer for the Merchants' and Farmers' Bank of Haversham. In time, he was presented one of those three-sided, walnut, felt-bottomed, brass-fronted, desktop nameplates with classic Olde English engraviture that read, Donald R. Black, Vice-President. And in truth, he did work hard, and in that sense did earn a healthy share of the title. But the truth would be less than complete in the telling if one failed to admit that it didn't hurt his promotional opportunities that one of the Merchants' and Farmers' Bank's largest and most valued depositors happened to be Americus Black.

Chapter 13

Jock Dejohnette inked in the frame in which the Retributor emerges from the alleyway. In the background, the glow of the burning BMW casts the elongated shadow of the fleeing punk against the brick facade of a dark building in mid-renovation. Jock reached for his red pen. He worked completely in black ink, but in every seventh frame, Jock added one small touch of color—a single green leaf clinging to the limb of a tree; the yellow eye of a gray alley cat. He got the idea from the child's red coat in *Schindler's List*, but he had adopted the small splash of color as what he considered his signature touch. In this frame, he colored the heart in the "I ♥ NY" logo on the Retibutor's black bag/mask a bold crimson.

He was almost finished with Issue #6 of *The Retributor*. He paused for a moment to think about his meager finances. He would only print a hundred copies of Issue #6, he decided. If he needed more—and he might; this might be the one, the one that catches on—he could always print more. He still had 423 copies of Issue #1. He had mailed out seventy-seven copies. Seventy-seven out of five hundred. Issues 2 through 5 had done little better, but for the last two issues, at least he had had the good sense to cut the run down to two hundred. He was sure he was paying too much for printing, but he couldn't figure out a way to break the cycle or the rule or whatever it was that seemed to say that in order to get the printing done for the small change that each copy should cost him, he had to print thousands of copies, but in order to justify printing thousands of copies, he had to have thousands of orders, but without major financial backing, he had to start small and build his readership, but starting small meant small printing orders and the smaller the printing order, the higher the cost per copy. He hated the financial end of trying to do something creative. He still thought his plan was a good one— to post the first couple of pages of each new issue on his website to tempt visitors to order the complete issue. He had gotten hits to his website, but not the thousands—much less the hundreds of thousands—the way it had played out in his head. His website also offered the Retributor tee-shirt he had designed—black with the Retributor's signature mark splashed across the chest—a scarlet *R*, the backstrap of the letter formed by a jagged lightning bolt. Initially, he offered them for $20. But he was not set up to accept credit cards, so those sales were skimpy, too. He had cut the price in half—a break-even proposition for him—reasoning that the shirts were a promotional tool—they didn't have to make money—but they were doing no promoting folded there in their boxes stacked in the corner of the room. *I'm just not a businessman*, he thought.

What he was, in his own mind, was, by nature, an artist, and by necessity, a kind of Robin Hood. The only way to underwrite his self-publishing enterprise was to steal from the rich—

defined as anyone who had more money than he had—and at that endeavor he had discovered he had a talent that rivaled his talent with pen and ink. He worked through a series of temporary staffing agencies, and never worked at any one place more than about a week. He preferred to work at locations where there were large numbers of female workers, and his temp job of choice was something that involved distributing mail. It only took him a couple of days to pick out the women who left their purses unattended in their offices or cubicles. He only took cash and the occasional piece of jewelry, and then he was gone—on to the next job and the next batch of careless office workers. *It'll teach them to be more careful*, he told himself. He considered it almost a public service.

It was as he working on Issue #4—the one in which the Retributor taught a lesson to reckless drivers—that Jock decided he needed to *see* the scenes through the eyes of his character. He had watched the young man racing through the streets of the neighborhood, burning rubber from one stop light to the next, drawing the kind attention to himself that would eventually earn him a visit from the comic book crusader. For two nights, the black-clothed figure tested the sensitivity of the Mercedes E320's alarm system as it was parked in front of the large house where the speed demon lived. *Nice house, nice car*, the shadowy figure thought, *it's a shame his parents gave him everything except a little consideration for others.* On the third night, inside his black bag, the dark visitor carried another bag which contained three small cans of spray paint—red, white, and yellow—and a small cheap plastic bottle which came from a hair treatment kit. The thin-walled plastic bottle was filled with gasoline. He also carried a broomstick. Quickly, quietly, delicately—he worked with the spray paint to transform the front of the car into an outlandish clown face. Across the trunk of the car, he left the painted message: "Drive like a fool; look like a fool. *R*." The signature R was the lightning bolt R of the Retributor. Finally, he slipped the plastic bottle into the tailpipe of the vehicle. With the broomstick, he pushed the bottle inside as far as the catalytic converter. Then, he went home, slipped into bed, and set the alarm to allow him three hours of sleep. He didn't want to miss the show when his handiwork was discovered. At six a.m., Jock took up his position on a bus stop bench across the street and a short distance away from the smiling clown car. He opened his newspaper and sipped his coffee and waited. Around 6:45, the man who was surely the father of the young man came out of the house. When the man saw the car, he seemed more confused than anything—he started toward the car, turned and headed back to the house, turned again and started back toward the car, then stopped and simply stared. After a minute, he walked back inside the house. A few minutes later, the man re-emerged with the sleepy-eyed young man who drove the car. The young man was dressed in a tee-shirt and sweatpants. When the young man saw the car, he swore loudly, "Son of a bitch!" Though he couldn't hear all of the conversation, Jock was amused to watch the father and son curse and speculate on who might have done such a thing. Finally, the father flipped open his cell phone and made a call. *Ah,* Jock thought, *now come the police.* But no police showed up. Instead, the young man went into the house and came back a short time later, this time fully dressed. The father mentioned something about insurance and the young man got in the car and revved the engine. *Race it some more*, thought Jock, *it'll heat that catalytic converter all the quicker.* Jock rose and began walking up the street, headed in the same direction the car was facing. The Mercedes peeled away from the curb and roared the half-block to the stop light, where the young man sat and impatiently revved the engine. Jock continued down the sidewalk. He looked down the street and observed that he could see five traffic lights before the road curved. The Mercedes made it to the fourth light before Jock saw the flames spew out the rear of the car. The driver's door flew open, and Jock watched the young man stomp around in the street, cursing, before another motorist stopped and said something to him, after which the young man ran to the sidewalk, pulled out his own cell phone and made a call. Jock watched the flames engulf the Mercedes. A couple of minutes later, he heard the siren of the fire truck. He smiled, crossed the street, and began to walk home, already picturing a frame in which the red light atop a fire truck was the only flash of color.

Chapter 14

The series of events that led eventually to the devouring of Donald Rayfield Black's character by the horrible dragon of small-town morality had begun nearly two years earlier with a comment whispered in Don's ear by nineteen-year-old Leslie Sue Sutter: "I like the way you smell. Sexy. In a clean and strong kind of way."

At first, Don was merely confused by the comment. He didn't wear aftershave or cologne. "It's Palmolive," he replied. And it was. Palmolive soap. Palmolive shaving cream. Then the delivery of the comment—the proximity and the volume—wafted over him like an exotic perfume itself, and he felt his face flush and his breath quicken slightly. Leslie Sue Sutter, even at nineteen, was no apprentice at the art of seduction; she was already honing her skills, trying new twists and variations.

Leslie—she pronounced it with a definite "S," rather than a "Z"—Sue Sutter—she pronounced the first syllable of her last name with the short "U"—plenty of people had already observed that it rhymed with "slut"—Slutter—was one of those women born, it seemed, with an aura of sexuality about her. She could pull off most seductions with nothing more than her eyes and her lips. For more challenging encounters she might stir in a toss of her yellow gold hair or a short, hypnotizing walk across the room. But there was more. Much, much more. She had the kind of breasts that publishers of men's magazines kept in a glass case in their right temporal lobes as the standard against which would-be centerfolds were measured. She wore them like she was being led around by them. They were advertising overkill in the same league as an "Ice Cold Beer" neon sign in the window of the only bar in Death Valley in July.

But among all that sexuality, there was a hint of sadness that lurked like that red and white striped hat in a "Find Waldo" puzzle—a flash of something that you knew was there and was out of place, but was difficult to spot. Until you'd spotted it, of course. And then it was difficult to blind yourself to.

There are people who have lots of sex for all the right reasons. Because they really, really enjoy it. Because they have huge appetites for pleasure— receiving it and giving it. And there are people who have lots of sex for all the wrong reasons. It's a form of self-loathing and self-debasement. It's something they are doing *to* themselves, as opposed to something they are doing *for* themselves. Their various partners are little more than instruments they use to gouge out new places within themselves for the sadness to hide. Leslie Sue Sutter's sadness needed lots of hiding places.

A few years down the road, one of Leslie Sue's acquaintances would say to someone in a bar: "Wanna hear something really sad? I have this friend, Leslie Sue, and we were playing this game at a party, and she drew this question that said,

'Describe yourself in one word.' ... And what she said was 'tits.'"

Chapter 15

"I don't know how to have this conversation." Katie Frye wanted to reach out and hold Casey's face in her two hands and look into his eyes so deeply and so purely that he would be able to see the truth without her having to say a word. Instead, she turned away, walked to the refrigerator, and took out a bottle of pinot grigio. Casey watched her squeak out the cork that had been stuck back into the mouth of the opened bottle and pour herself a glass. *She won't look at me*, he thought.

"I don't expect you to say much," he said. "I just need to tell you about it. I've already decided. 'Course, I'd love to hear anything to have to say about it 'cause...I don't know...I'm not sure about.... Truth is—I'm a little scared, Mom."

Her breath caught, and her eyes welled before she could stop them. She took a deep breath and then a sip of her wine. She blotted her eyes with a paper towel, put on a smile, and turned back to her son.

"Of course you're scared. Who wouldn't be? I'm scared *for* you. Not as much as I should be, probably, about the cancer, because you're going to beat it. I know that. I know that in my heart. The operation's a little scary because, well, operations are always scary. I don't know why; they just are. ... I'm scared, Casey, because this cancer, this operation...is making me have to tell you something I thought was over and done. And I don't know what it's going to do to you."

"*Do* to me?"

"To us."

"I don't know what you mean, Mom."

"I know, baby." *And you were never supposed to know*, she thought to herself. "Whoever's in charge of the secrets of the universe is one sick puppy. Sit down, baby. And try to stay sitting down for a few minutes, all right?" Casey sat on the sofa. She sat in her chair—the one she sat in to watch TV and to drink her coffee and to do her crossword puzzle on Sunday mornings. She took another sip of wine and set her glass on the coffee table and just looked at him.

"Well, say something."

"What would happen if you couldn't have this transplant operation?"

"I've already told you, Mom. I'm *going* to have the transplant."

"I know. But what if you couldn't? What then?"

"I'd...well, I'd be...I'd never be able...."

"...to have children."

"I wouldn't be a whole *man*! Why are you asking me this? What are you doing?!"

"I don't want to make you uncomfortable, baby, and I'm not trying to pry into your sex life, believe me. I just need to know. If you couldn't have this operation...you'd be *alive*, right? There are things they can do now as far as being able to have sex—you could still get married. If you and Debbie

71

want children, you can adopt. There are even things they can do now before the operation so that she can have kids by artificial insemination. *Your* kids."

"I don't understand! I want this operation. Dr. Strejc says he can do it. He says he can make it work. He's so sure that he makes me sure. Why are you doing this? Why are you trying to undermine that confidence?

"I'm not trying to undermine anything! I'm not. It's just that the key to this whole thing working out the way it's supposed to work out seems to be the donor match. Isn't that right? Isn't that what you were telling me?"

"Yes. But Dr. Strejc says that Dad is my best chance for a match. What are you saying? That you think Dad'll change his mind? What? We talked. Dr. Strejc talked to him. I told you all this."

"Damn!" she stood quickly and turned. "Damn, damn, damn, damn, *damn*!" She looked around like she had come to a dead-end in a maze and didn't know where to turn.

"Mom...you've lost me. I don't get it."

"... Your dad—Fred Frye—is not your father."

"Not my—? What're you saying? I'm...adopted?"

"No." She said it softly.

"'Cause I can't believe you would wait until—"

"No." This time firmly. "No; that's not what I'm saying."

"Well, then, I really don't get it, Mom. I mean, that doesn't make any sen—. ... Oh, my God."

"He doesn't know."

"How could he *not know*? What does that mean?"

"He thinks...you thought...the whole world thought he was. Your father."

"So you're saying...who? You what—had an affair or something? I don't believe this. I don't believe *you*. Why would you say something like that? Why would you make up some shit like that?"

"Make *up*? You think I would make *up* something like this? I'd rather tear my heart out with my bare hands and hand it to you than have to have this conversation! But I won't have you go into an operation thinking everything's fine, everything going to be all right, when *I* know it can't work. I can't let you do that. I...I'm...so...so..."

"Sorry?"

"Yes. And ashamed. And hurt and afraid and so many other things that I can't sort them all out right now."

"You're *sorry*? ... And *he doesn't know*? ... And *you're* sorry. ... And I'm...."

There is no silence like the silence that settles on the survivors of a world that has crashed down around them.

After a few moments, she picked up the wine glass, drained it, and set it back down on the coffee table. Casey walked over, picked up the glass, and flung it against the wall in front of them. A small shard of the shattering glass ricocheted and cut Katie's cheek, and her hand flew instinctively to her face. It was a small wound—just a nick, really—but when she lowered her hand, there was blood on it. Casey didn't even notice. He had already turned and walked to the door. She put her hand back to her cheek just as he turned around.

"They haven't even done the testing yet," he said. "When they did, they would have probably just said it wasn't the match they had hoped it would be. ... So who is it? Are you at least going to tell me who my real father is? Do I at least get that much out of the deal?"

"His name was Lennie Lupo. I don't know where he is. I don't know if he's even still alive."

Casey turned and walked out, closing the door behind him. Katie dropped her hand from her cheek, then looked at it again. There was more blood. In a way, it was a relief to bleed.

Chapter 16

In flagrante delicto: caught in the very act of "doing it." The only way it could have possibly been worse, Don Black reasoned, was if it had been *in flagrare delicto*: actually *on fire* when caught in the act. On the courthouse steps, perhaps...with his parents watching...along with a reunion of his fifth grade classmates, all pointing and laughing. *Yes*, he thought, *yes—that would have been worse. But that's about the* only *way it could have been worse.*

It's difficult to say whether or not Don Black would have ever actually strayed into the Adulterers' Club had Leslie Sue Sutter not come to work that summer of '82 in the bank's small Operations Center which Don oversaw. There was certainly potential for cheating—the seeds of self-justification were ripe to the bursting point within his mind. But whether or not he would have ever actually acted upon the thoughts in his head—well, that would be an iffy bit of prognostication at best.

The seeds had lain dormant since his wife Beth's teary confession of infidelity had burst forth in the midst of a stress-filled week during which, among other things, she had wrecked her car in her haste to get to the hospital where her father had been taken following what turned out to be a mild heart attack. There is apparently absolutely no way to predict what chamber of secrets that accumulated stress may dynamite without warning. When the explosion was over, though, he had learned this much: The affair had been brief—"It was only three or four times." It had happened more than three years prior. It was over, definitely over. No—she would not tell him who the man was. The thing from among the sketchy details of the confessed indiscretion that Don's mind eventually latched onto and—finding itself incapable of satisfactorily reconciling the fragment of information—planted in a little out-of-the-way patch of gray matter to see what would sprout...was the admission that the dirty deed was done "three or four times." Three. Or four. Was it three...or was it four? The more his mind played with the little detail, the more puzzling it became. Remembering whether it was three times or four times should be a fairly easy matter. *I mean*, he thought, *it's not like we're dealing with the question, "Now, how many times, exactly, have I passed that mailbox down at the corner? Was it six thousand and twenty-*seven *or was it six thousand and twenty-*eight*?" Jeez, I just don't remember.* If you went to all the trouble to sneak away from your spouse...and get naked...and fuck some stranger...it seemed to him, you would remember whether you did that three times...or four times.

What began to sprout was the decision that it had been four times—definitely four—and the notion that *he* now had four "pieces of strange" banked, so to speak. It wasn't really spiteful or vengeful. It was more a balancing of the books. A sense of entitlement. He had four pieces of extramarital nookey coming to him. In dim corners of his mind, little committees met and worked out the finer points of his strange-pussy trust fund and hammered out answers to their own questions.

Now, when she said three or four times, did that mean—

Excuse me, Mr. Chairman—I don't mean to interrupt—but I believe we decided that the number we're working with here is four.

You're right. I apologize. Okay. When she said four times, did that mean she actually performed the sex act four times? Or...did the number four simply quantify the number of meetings—any one of which or all of which could have involved having sex more than once? So I guess the question is: Does Don get to perform the sex act with some strange woman or women four times—period, or does he get to surreptitiously meet with said strange woman or women on four different occasions and get as much pussy as he can on each of those occasions?

And what about blowjobs? Do they count?

Only if the blowjob is carried out to fruition, I would think. I mean, surely, a blowjob that's only foreplay doesn't count, right?

Oh, no.

Absolutely not.

So can we agree on that? All in favor of blowjobs which do not result in orgasm NOT being debited against the said number—four or whatever we end up deciding on—indicate by saying "Aye."

Aye.

Aye.

Aye.

Motion carried. Let's proceed.

And on and on it went. It might have gone on forever, purely as a kind of mental exercise, had not Leslie Sue Sutter jiggled her way into the Merchants' and Farmers' Bank of Haversham that summer.

It was on the second occasion of Don Black's sexual adventures in Leslie-Land that he was "caught in the act" by none other than Pillsbury Sinclair, the President of the Merchants' and Farmers' Bank of Haversham and Trudy Dufrense, Mr. Sinclair's secretary of some twenty-odd years. Upon Don's first glimpse of Leslie's exquisitely perfect breasts, the Quantification Sub-committee of the Rules Committee Governing Equitable Access to the Strange-Pussy Trust had voted unanimously that the number four referred only to "sessions of indeterminate length" during which time "anything, including frequency and duration of sexual acts, was fair game." It was a decision that all of his body parts applauded.

Don had made his first withdrawal from the trust in the form of a hasty, but New-Years-Eve-pyrotechnic-grade blowjob in his car, the Friday evening Leslie had batted her eyes and told him her "mean ol' car" wouldn't start and asked him to give her a ride home. Though she did open her blouse and unclasp her bra and allow her fantasy fodder tits to spill out and fill his hands to overflowing, he never made it to Pussy Junction—a shortcoming he regretted from the moment she bounced from his car, purred "Mmmm. Thanks for the ride," and disappeared into the back door of her house. Even his most lascivious imaginings about how he was going to compensate for that missed opportunity did not prepare him for the gills-deep hook Leslie sank into his libido the next Friday afternoon.

All week, he had considered the logistics of it—the where and when. Right there in the bank was not on his list. Not until Leslie stopped at his desk that Friday afternoon.

He sat at his desk, an office supply catalog in his left hand, his right arm propped on the armrest of his chair. When she walked up beside him and reached down and took his right hand, he instinctively looked everywhere but at her, to make sure no one was around to see them. That's why he wasn't looking when she grasped his wrist and pulled his hand up beneath her skirt and between her parted legs. When his hand touched her, he felt his head swim.

When he looked up at her, he saw that she had tied her hair into two ponytails with ribbon. She pouted her lips, and said, "I shaved it." Then in an "animal crackers in my soup" voice, "You don't think it'll make me look too much like a widdle girl, do you?" His willpower, along with his good sense, unraveled like a cheap sweater. If she had asked for one of his kidneys at that moment, he would have handed her his letter opener. With his left hand. His right hand was going nowhere. Finally, she stepped back, leaving his hand feeling moist and warm and strangely orphaned. "I'm having a widdle twouble with some of the paperwork. Do you think you can stay a widdle late and help me?" she cooed. His head nodded all by itself. It wasn't until sometime after she had disappeared from the room that he realized that he was still nodding.

It was a long time before Don even considered what purpose might have accounted for Mr. Sinclair and Ms. Dufrense's late presence on the premises. He couldn't get past the moment, flash-burned on his memory, when he had heard Ms. Dufrense gasp and Mr. Sinclair clear his throat.

"Oh, daddy, daddy. It's so big, daddy! It's so big in—" And that's the moment—the moment he heard the gasp and the throat-clearing. "—my widdle puddy!"

And suddenly it wasn't "so big"...anymore.

There's just no graceful way to greet your boss and your boss' secretary when you discover them standing behind you, as you stand there naked with a nineteen-year-old equally naked girl on the end of your dick and bent over your desk. Fortunately, Mr. Sinclair and Ms. Dufrense filled the vacuum with just the precise measures of righteous indignation and shocked dismay, so that the awkwardness of the moment quickly gave way to frantic scrambling for pieces of clothing and gauzy swatches of propriety. The first intelligible piece of information to successfully penetrate the fog of shock and slish vapors was Pillsbury Sinclair's pronouncement, "You *will* be in first thing Monday morning, won't you...?" For a slippery second, Don mistook the words for a complete statement, one tinged with the faint assertion that "we'll get through this somehow," but it quickly became clear that the words were merely the left jabs to set up the right hook, "...to clean out your desk."

Chapter 17

"Tell me when you're going to come." Her voice was breathy.

"What?" It was one of those automatic things that you say when you heard perfectly well what was said, but the question is startled out of you.

"Tell me when you're going to come." Her breathing was, if anything, quicker and more shallow.

Lennie Lupo had known his share of women, but he had never heard a woman—at least not one who didn't work in the porn industry—actually use the word *come* in its sexual context out loud. It was both startling and exciting. If he had been asked to come up with a description of the woman whom he might envision panting out the phrase, nothing about her—at least nothing from the first impression he formed when he met her three hours earlier—would have been made the line-up. But this woman—Katie, she had said her name was—was proving to be a one-woman surprise party.

"Okay," he said.

"Can you pull out?"

"What?" *Damn!* He thought—*I said it again.*

"When you come. Can you pull out?"

"Yes." His answer was forced to escape between his ragged breaths. Even that part of the brain that controls such autonomic functions seemed to be awash in the increasingly demanding tide of slishy sensations rising from their coupling.

"I want to get on top." He couldn't decide if it was a plea or a demand, but he rolled to his left side, taking her with him. She took over in mid-roll, pushing him onto his back. When she pushed back, then sat up and arched her back, she bent his erection, trapped in the tight, slick clutch of her vagina, to the precise angle that separates exquisite from excruciating. It must have been the exact angle that she was looking for because she locked her legs and began a steady, tortuously titillating ride up and down the unbearably engorged stalk of his penis.

"Oh, God," she gurgled, "I'm gonna come. I'm gonna come so hard."

The words ran like electricity through his blood. He fought for control.

"Oh. Oh. Oh, oh, oh, oh, oh, oh," each syllable punctuated a jerk of her upper body; then she jammed herself down and back onto him and froze. Her mouth formed one last silent *oh*, and he could have sworn he actually felt the blood-fizz of her orgasm swarm around his trapped organ. It was too much.

"Now," he gasped, desperately trying to hold back.

"Say it," she said, still pressed fully back onto his impaling cock.

"I have to come!" The words burst from his throat as he felt the dam burst within him. It was too late to say more. All he could do was roar as he felt her lift off of him. In one liquid motion she slipped down, gripped his penis, slick with her own juices, and pressed it into the warm fleshy cushion of her breast. He was sure his legs themselves were dissolving and rushing out in the pearly flood.

When the sparkle-throbs fizzled out, he looked down and found her looking up at him. His weak, lopsided grin met her smoky smile halfway, and they both began to laugh because the moment was too good for words to do it justice.

It was the first time he'd laughed like that since Joanne.

Chapter 18

The fall from grace in a small town is not like Wiley Coyote's fall from that cartoonish cliff—Oops! Uh-oh! Zip! Thud! It's more like a fall from the top of a tall, sturdy pine tree—a few bone-crunching collisions with larger branches along the way and a steady, stinging, general lashing by the needley population all the way down. It is not an event marked by clear thinking, especially on the part of the faller.

In Don's mind, the only thing to do was to go home, pack his clothes, confess his sin to Beth—thereby beating the forces of righteous indignation to the punch—and walk out the door. He would try to make the best life he could with Leslie Sue. It was a genuine jolt, therefore, when he hit that first branch and it cut him a flip.

The whole thing took on a surreal quality when he arrived at Leslie Sue's house. At first, he thought he had knocked on the wrong door. A teenaged guy wearing a Kiss tee-shirt and camouflage pants opened the door, "Yeah?"

When Don asked for Leslie Sue, the kid hollered, and she came to the door, eating from a box of Cheese-Its.

"Oh, hi."

The kid in the tee-shirt wandered back into the same room from which Leslie Sue had emerged. She offered no introduction and no explanation.

"Sorry about you losing your job and all.

Bummer, huh?"

"Bummer?"

"Do you think I'm in trouble, too? Guess I'll find out Monday when I go in, huh?"

Don groped around for a handle on the moment. "I, uh, left my wife. I told her what happened—sort of—and I, uh, left."

"Oh, wow. *Real* bummer. So you think you'll get a divorce and all? My parents got a divorce when I was, like, thirteen."

"Uh, are we—. Are you—." He wasn't even sure how to put his confusion into words.

She offered him the box, "You want some Cheese-Its?"

"What? No. Listen—I'm a little confused. I think I must've misunderstood something. Can we...talk?"

"Sure. Oh, hey—could you do us a favor first? Could you run up to the Majik Market and get a couple of six-packs of beer?"

"Beer?"

"Yeah. That would be so cool. Sometimes Bobby's brother buys it for us, but he's off at, like, Myrtle Beach or somewhere."

"You want me to go buy you beer?"

"It's no big deal. But, I mean, if you don't want to or anything..."

"No, no. I'll, uh...I'll be right back."

Don walked to his car, drove off, and just kept driving. He got on the interstate and headed toward Atlanta. Just outside of Atlanta, he stopped at a gas station, filled up and bought two six-packs of Michelob Light and a box of Cheese-Its. Then he drove across the street to a Comfort Inn and checked in. He didn't leave the room until Sunday night.

Chapter 19

Sometimes when the phone rang at ten o'clock at night, he remembered *the* phone call. It was no longer an actual physical sensation of anxiety's icy finger touching him; now, it was more like a flicker of something in the corner of his eye. Several years before *the* phone call, Lennie's own parents had died only a year apart, each snatched quickly and mercifully from this plane of existence by the hand of heart attack. Perhaps that was part of why he knew it was so important to Joanne to spend as much time as she could at the nursing facility where her stricken mother was clinging so tenaciously to the ragged and soiled hem of Life's nightgown. Maybe it would make it easier for her mother to relax and let go if Joanne sat and held her hand and placed her mother's smooth, scared palm on her swollen belly to feel the baby, a girl, due in a month, ready to step into her grandmother's place in the long line of generations. Two faint heartbeats played tag through the one strong heartbeat that connected them. That's where she had been and was on the way home from that night when the phone rang at ten o'clock, and a voice said that there had been an accident. And the next day, Joanne's mother relaxed and let go. And the three of them—Joanne's mother, Joanne, and the baby—strolled off into eternity to get to know each other all over again. And Lennie Lupo was left behind with the ringing phones.

Chapter 20

The next year of Don Black's life was a patchwork quilt of embarrassing moments, uncomfortable situations, legal unpleasantries, and degrading conversations with family, acquaintances, and former business associates. And yet, he was oddly detached from most of it, insulated it seemed by the general malaise into which he had slipped. It seemed, somehow, to Don that he spent the year living underwater, wandering around in one of those deep sea diving suits—life swirling around him, predators swooping nearby, his senses of touch, hearing, and seeing numbed, muted, and wavy. Eventually, his father, the ever-steady Americus Black, told him—didn't *ask* him, but *told* him—that he would come to work at the Chevrolet dealership. So, he began spending his days there, the workaday activities and questions and demands beginning to peck at and slowly pick to shreds the diving suit, returning to him his physical senses, and forcing him at least to come up for air. And one year gave way to another.

One of the more demeaning aspects of working at AB Chevrolet was the sudden visitations by his sister Abbie. Abbie Black Flagg now, having married Julius Flagg, a lawyer who specialized, apparently, in legal justifications as to why people should pay him while he played golf. The skull-and-crossbones image that her name conjured up for everyone else seemed completely lost on her. Abbie operated as sort of a Commando Office Manager. She would make lightning raid appearances two or three times a week, slash and hack her way through the office staff, carve a scarlet "I" for "incompetence" into the forehead of a random employee or two, then stand in the open doorway of Don's office and rail at his "uselessness." For all of this, she received a paycheck about double Don's and a peck on the cheek, *always*, from their father.

When Americus Black's long overdue stroke finally bitch-slapped him into an incontinent, paralyzed, drooling and babbling bed monkey, it was no surprise that Abbie Black Flagg took charge with all the grace and compassion of Bluebeard conducting an IRS audit. What was so belittling was that Don had to find out about her plans from Shorty Conklin who ran a gas station in town and whose youngest boy worked as a mechanic at the Chevrolet dealership.

"Gonna be strange ridin' by there and not seein' that big ol' AB up there on the sign."

"What are you talking about, Shorty? We're not doing anything with the sign."

"I hear'd the new owners was gonna call it Chevy City."

"What new owners?! What the hell're you talking about?"

"'S what my boy tole me. Shoot, I figgered you know'd all about it. That's gon' be twelve-seb'ndee-five."

Chapter 21

He considered himself a genius. Jock had always considered himself a genius. It was how he saw himself. Not as one of those child intellectual prodigies who graduates college at age twelve, though he told himself that he *could* have if he had applied himself. He was bright, though he had not distinguished himself academically. That, too, was a choice he had made, he told himself. A creative genius. In his own mind, that was who he truly was. And a true creative genius simply couldn't be bothered with petty academic accomplishments. Somehow, though, he believed, genius bled over into almost all other intellectual endeavors. Certain episodes of *Jeopardy* validated his belief. When he watched the show, he often knew the answers. He could be a *Jeopardy* champion, he believed, if he was ever given the opportunity. Even when he didn't know the answers right off, as soon as a contestant supplied the correct answer, he recognized it and said to himself, "Oh, yeah; that's right. I knew that." Though his true genius coursed through the creative realm, he saw it as overflowing the banks of its channel, so that all of his other intellectual undertakings were fed by those fertile waters. Genius. He wore the title like Brando wore his hat in *The Wild One*.

That is why the laughter cut him so quickly and so deeply. Clancy's Keep was an Irish pub, indistinguishable from other Irish pubs in the city, except for one item. Behind the bar, all alone on a shelf against a mirrored section of the back wall, an old bottle sat as if enshrined. It was a Hennessy's Cognac bottle, circa 1794. In terms of the bottle's contents, its liquid spirits had long since departed, and yet, to Solon Simpson, the bar's owner, as well as to the pub's cadre of regulars, the bottle was anything but empty. Above the bottle, in arched gold letters, was painted the legend "The Genius of Clancy's Keep."

Though occasionally one of the regulars whose luck was in need of turning would buy one for the Genius, mostly they depended on unsuspecting strangers, especially tourists who wandered in, to spring for the sacrificial shots to the Genius. The appeal to "buy one for the Genius" could be dangled before a visitor so that it fairly dripped with lilt and light-hearted blarney or so that it hovered in menacing fog and hung there shrouded in implied cursed consequences for noncompliance, depending on how welcome the newcomer's company was to the assembled locals.

The seed of the story was this: The bottle was among the first shipment of Hennessy's to the new America in 1794. Aboard that same ship was a stowaway—Ian Clancy—a man wrongly accused of conspiring against the British crown, who had been sentenced to the gallows, but who had escaped and had hidden away on the ship to America. When he was discovered, the captain pressed him into service to pay his passage, but he fell ill with a fever. Afraid he might infect the rest of the crew, the captain locked him away in a lower hold where he withered away to near-death. As he lay burning with fever on the straw cot that would be his deathbed, he told the one crew member, a cabin boy—Solon Simpson's great-great-great grandfather—who was assigned to afford him what little attendance the captain would allow—that in exchange for a taste of good Irish spirits he would offer his own immortal spirit to serve and guard over the man who did him that last good deed. The young Simpson stole a bottle of Hennessy's from the shipment—the very bottle that stood on the shelf, in fact—and sneaked it in to the dying man. The next day, as the cabin boy came to check on Clancy, he found him lying still, clutching the bottle in his hand. As the boy reached for the bottle, the man opened his eyes and said: "Take care, lad, with that bottle. For though they will give my body this day to the deep blue sea, I have stoppered my soul in this bottle. Carry it to freedom in the new land, and it will evermore watch over you and yours. Do it the occasional good turn by offering it a taste of good Irish spirits, and it will do you a good turn, as well." And then he died. When the ship arrived in America, young Simpson stayed and eventually opened a pub and prospered. And through the generations, the Simpsons had passed along the pub and the old bottle and the spirit of Ian Clancy, whose thirst was never quenched and whose promise to do a good turn for whoever bought him a drink had never failed. But...deny him a drink when he's thirsty, they said, and he would come and take a long drink from the well of what good fortune you had coming in this life and leave you wanting.

Generally, the newcomer—even if he or she just viewed the purchase as payment for the bit of entertainment—bought the Genius a drink. Solon Simpson would ring a bell that was mounted on the wall behind the bar, pour a shot from a new bottle of Hennessy's and set it on the shelf beside the old bottle. After a few moments, during which time the group at the bar typically fell silent and, along with the buyer, just watched the drink sitting there as if it might miraculously empty itself, Solon would say, "What's that, Ian? Had enough? Help you out? For sure, lad—that's what I'm here for." And he would pick up the shot glass, raise it in a toast to the bottle, and suck it down. And the regulars would laugh and clap and cheer.

The night that Jock wandered into Clancy's Keep, the pub was crowded. Several tourists had already bought the Genius a shot, but that was before Jock arrived, so he had not heard the story. Because it was so crowded, everyone assumed he had. When he squeezed up to the bar and ordered a beer, Solon drew the draught and set it before him, took the ten dollar bill and made change, but when he put the bills on the bar, he kept his hand on top of them while he looked at Jock and said, "I don't believe *you've* bought the Genius a drink yet, have you, lad?"

Jock glanced up and down the bar at the

faces of the regulars, then looked back at Solon. "Yeah. I believe I just bought a beer for the closest thing to genius I see in *this* place." When he grabbed at the corner of the bills, Solon pressed his beefy palm down harder, pinning the bills to the bar. The corner of one of the bills tore away, leaving Jock with a ragged triangle pinched between his thumb and forefinger. "Oh, I get it," Jock said, "*you're* the fuckin' genius." He flipped the piece of torn bill onto the bar and said, "Well, here you go, genius—that's your fuckin' tip."

Solon remained cemented to the spot and smiled. The regulars at the bar hooted and chorused, "Whoa-ho-ho!" They loved a newcomer with a smartass attitude like a pack of hounds loved a rabbit in their midst.

"Do you even know what a genius *is*, lad? I'll bet you everything you've got here on the bar against all you can drink tonight that you don't," Solon taunted.

Jock rankled to the challenge to his intellect, but it seemed too easy. He suspected a trick. "According to *whom*?" he shot back, emphasizing the *whom* as if to warn them of his intellectual prowess by demonstrating he knew the difference between the subjective and the objective cases of the pronoun and he was not afraid to use them correctly.

With his other hand, Solon reached beneath the bar and produced a worn desk edition dictionary and dropped it on the counter. "Why, Mr. Webster, lad. You're familiar with his works, I'm sure."

"Oh, I get it. Word for word? No, thanks."

"Not word for word, lad. Your own words'll do nicely. Anywhere in the ballpark. Primary definition. Preferred usage. Simple as that. 'Course if you don't *know*...."

"Intellectually gifted. An extremely smart and/or talented individual," Jock said, carefully articulating each word, as if for the benefit of a both hearing-impaired and mentally slow listener. "Though it probably doesn't say it in there, I would add, 'unlike any among the staff and usual patrons of this establishment.' Close enough?"

"Well, I don't know, lad. Why don't you look it up and tell us. Definition number one, I believe, is the preferred usage. Isn't that the way it works?"

Jock flipped through the pages until he came to it. He found it on the page that covered *general* to *genre. Genius: a guardian or tutelary spirit; an attendant spirit, esp. one with a fondness for social enjoyment. A jinn.*

The crowd around him saw the exact moment his face fell, then clouded over, and they erupted in laughter. Solon closed his fist around the bills on the bar. Someone shouted above the noise, "Why don't you look up 'sucker bet' next, laddie?"

There's a phrase the French have—*esprit de l'escalier*. It refers to the clever rejoinder to the public insult, or the brilliantly witty remark that comes into your mind only after you have left the party. "Yeah! That's what I *should* have said!" That kind of thing. Regardless of the way he pronounced his name, Jock was never very good at French, though at the moment he could have been the bereted poster boy for the phrase.

Jock left his beer sitting on the bar, wheeled away, and began pushing his way toward the exit. Behind him, a bell rang and the crowd laughed and cheered. As he shoved the door open, the cold outside air stung his burning face. The bar sounds faded as he walked briskly down the street, but the laughter stayed with him, well beyond the range of normal hearing.

Chapter 22

The marriage of Katie Wentz and Lt. Fred Frye, USN, in 1975, had been a good match in many ways. They were compatible on many levels. Having grown up in Norfolk, Katie had come to realize the importance of the Navy to her hometown. Her parents raised her to appreciate that service to one's country was a good and honorable thing, but they had also instilled in her a common sense, realistic wariness of becoming "the girl in the port" of Norfolk. "Navy dress whites and wedding dress whites really just don't wear all that well together in the long run," her mother used to warn. The only reason Lt. Fred Frye, USN, was able to get his foot in the door at all was that his Lt. and his USN were trumped by his DDS. He was a dentist. With plans for a nice civilian dental practice as soon as his Navy days were done. He came from a nice family and appreciated the finer material things that a successful dental practice could make possible. And in truth, he was a pretty good guy. He just hadn't really been passionate about anything since they installed a Foosball table in the game room of his dorm in undergraduate school.

Barely two years into their marriage, Katie was not pleased to learn that she would have to give up her job as a speech pathologist to follow her husband to his new duty station. There was some consolation in the fact that the new duty station was Key West Naval Air Station.

Traps are among the shape-shiftingest of things. There are rat traps and bear traps. Bungee traps. There are speed traps. Tourist traps. Rattletraps. There are drain traps and sand traps. Trap sets. Trapshoots. Trapdoors. Even trapezoids. And there are thinking traps. Lines of thought that keep taking you down the same primrose path to the same discovery that there is no gazebo at the end. Over and over and over.

Key West can sweet-talk the most modest of curvy young women into a bikini. Key West *is* Bikini-town. The bikini is the uniform of the day. Every day. The rate of fire of a Vulcan machine gun is approximately 2000 rounds per minute. Curvy young women in bikinis bombard the brains of young men with thoughts of sex at only a slightly higher rate. Thoughts of sex sometimes lead to *actual* sex. Actual sex sometimes leads to pregnancy. Pregnancy is basically Kryptonite to bikinis. When you connect all the dots, you discover the outline of one of the sneakiest of traps.

Katie Frye liked the way she looked in a bikini. Lt. Fred Frye—not to mention every heterosexual male with working vision—liked the way Katie Frye looked in a bikini. Katie Frye in a bikini caused images of sex to run like an endless loop of tape in Fred Frye's head. And in the distance behind those images, images of little Fred Juniors and little Katies frolicked in a kiddie pool. Katie Frye did *not* like the way she imagined she looked in maternity clothes...standing at the end of a primrose path...with no gazebo in sight.

Chapter 23

He woke himself up laughing. And then the pure sweetness—of how happy that moment about which he had been dreaming was—flooded over him and it all became overwhelmingly sad. It was a sadness that had been locked in a place deep in his chest for a long time, and it tried to break out in a sob before he caught it and forced it back into its stony cell and slammed the door on it.

On his wedding day, Lennie Lupo's father had handed him the keys to an old Karmen Ghia convertible that he had restored. Frank Lupo—Lennie's father—moved through life in a zigzag pattern from one entrepreneurial failure to the next—drawn to glittery, foolish opportunity like a man lost in the desert is drawn to the mirage of an oasis. Between the failures, to keep food on the table, Frank was a pretty darn good mechanic. He would buy old cars or wrecks, fix them up, and sell them. One of his finer restorations had been the old Karmen Ghia. Unlike the other fixer-uppers, though, Frank had fixed a price in his head that simply wasn't negotiable, and so it had sat in his old carport waiting for the guy who was willing to meet that price. That's why, when Frank handed Lennie the keys on his wedding day, it was such a surprise. Lennie and his new bride Joanne had tooled around town with the top down, driven out into the country for a picnic, and spent one whole Saturday hand-washing and waxing the sleek curves of old Ghia.

The pounding on their front door jarred them awake the next Saturday morning. They couldn't imagine who could be at their door at 6:00 in the morning. Lennie had an old H&R .22 pistol that he kept in the nightstand drawer, and he handed it to Joanne, and told her to stay there while he went to the door. She huddled on her side of the bed—one hand on the telephone, the other hand holding the .22.

When Lennie cracked the door, his father didn't say "good morning" or "sorry to wake you up" or anything. He just said, "I need the keys to the Karmen Ghia."

"Dad," Lennie said, "what are you doing here? It's six o'clock in the morning. You scared us half to death."

Frank looked at him blankly. "Oh. Sorry. I need the keys to the Ghia."

"Why do you need the keys to the Ghia?" he asked, confused.

"I found a buyer in Atlanta," Frank said, "and I need to get it to him today."

"But, Dad," Lennie stammered, now even more confused, "that was our *wedding* gift!"

"The wedding was *two weeks* ago!" his father said, "I need the keys."

After his father left with the car, Lennie got his first close-up look at his new wife's complete range of emotions in rapid-fire succession. Joanne went from screaming laughter to utter tears to shrieking and cussing, complete with the firing of two rounds from the .22 into their dresser, which seemed to bring her back to the peals of laughter, all in a matter of minutes. Lennie finally managed to jump on board the runaway emotional express when it hit that last stretch of laughter, and together they collapsed among the sheets and the bed quilt in a fit of laughing that echoed through their small house, out the front door, down the block, and all the way into the dream that woke him, so far down the road. Laughter that pure would certainly live forever, even if the laughers didn't.

Woody got up, lit a cigarette, and walked to the window. He looked out and almost expected to see the laughter ricocheting from lightpole to lightpole, looking for some unsuspecting passerby to zap into sillydom. But there were no passersby, and the streetlights took their duties all too seriously, and the face semi-reflected in the window looked like it could use some more sleep...and some more laughter.

Chapter 24

Jock Dejohnette learned to draw early. He discovered that he had a natural talent, but that's not what kept him drawing. It was the fact that he could make the things and the people he drew do anything he wanted them to do. They only said what he allowed them to say. They never argued with him.

"Mama! Jock left the seat up on the commode again!"

"Jock—how many times have you been told about that toilet seat?"

"At least ten million, I'd say, Mama. He don't listen."

"Doesn't listen, Marie. Don't say don't."

"You just said don't."

"You know what I meant."

"He just doodles and daydreams; that's all he does."

In the first frame of the drawing, a teenaged girl with frizzy hair twisted her face into a spiteful sneer—her brow wrinkled, her eyes narrowed, her nose turned up, the nostrils flared and drawn upward and outward, her upper lip curled up and back from her teeth, the lower lip protruding in a hard ridge.

"Are you listening to me, young man? Put down that pen when I'm talking to you."

"It's a pencil; not a pen; and I think it's grown to his hand."

"I am handling this, Marie. When I want

your input, I'll ask for it."

"Ask for it, my foot."

"What did you say?"

"Nothing."

"Don't you 'nothing' me, missy. You sound just like that smart-mouthed so-called friend of yours, Janet."

"Jann*ette*. And at least I *have* friends."

In the second frame, a hand appeared just inside the left border. The girl's head tilted slightly so that curiosity flowed across her face to mix with the surprise in her eyes.

"Friends do not talk their friends into drinking alcohol. Especially when the friend is underage, and the alcohol is stolen."

"It wasn't alcohol; it was just beer."

"Beer is alcohol."

"Not like liquor."

"Yes, it *is*. Alcohol is alcohol, whether it's in vodka or liquor or beer."

"Ha!"

"What do you mean, 'ha'?"

"Vodka *is* liquor. You said 'vodka *or* liquor.' Vodka is just a *kind* of liquor."

"What are you—*proud* that you know the difference? If you would apply that enthusiasm for learning to algebra instead of 'I'll take Types of Liquor for 200, Alex,' maybe you wouldn't be building your circle of friends from high school drop-outs and losers."

"Exponential! Polynomial!"

"What is *that* supposed to mean? You have lost your mind, young lady."

"See? See?! Like *you* know anything about algebra."

In the third frame, the hand had clamped itself over the girl's mouth and nose. Her eyes were wild with panic, the veins in her temples swollen with fear and oxygen deprivation.

"With the way your attitude is going downhill, I don't think I want you seeing Miss Janet Junk-mouth anymore."

"Jann*ette*! And you can't tell me who to see and who not to see. It's a free country. People can go anywhere they want, including places where other people might *see* them. Even people who bitch about them."

"You will *not* use that kind of language in *my* house. You hear me?"

"Your house? Did *you* pay for it? I'm sorry—I thought *Daddy* was the one who had a job to make the money to do the *paying* around here. Daaad-dy?!"

"What?"

"Come here, please?"

"What for?"

"Just come here, please!"

"What for?"

"Please?! Just come in here a minute?"

"All right. I'm here. What?"

"Is this or is this not a free country?"

"That's right, missy—you won't use the

106

kind of language in front of your father that you think you can get away with with me, will you? She stood right there and for all intents and purposes called me the B word."

"What the hell is wrong with you two? If I wanted a cat fight, I'da baited the back porch with sardines! ... And *you*. Get that goddamn *drawin'* shit off my table."

"You hear what he said? *My* table. *His* table, *his* house."

In the fourth frame, the girl's eyes were fixed in a flat, dead stare. The side of her head had split open and oozed a thick river of pus, clogged with worms and dog turds and used condoms. Jock scooped up the sheets of drawing paper, his pencils, and the Grumbacher eraser, smiled to himself, and headed for his room.

Chapter 25

Well, Merry fucking Christmas to me, Katie Frye thought to herself. The radio was alternating Christmas songs with a countdown of the year's top hits. "New Kid in Town" was playing. She reached over and switched off the radio on the bedside table. If she heard "You Light Up My Life" one more time, she thought she might puke. And she knew it had to be coming.

She thought about the last argument she and her husband had had. Irony is just a literary term until it strolls into your bathroom while you're brushing your teeth, takes a piss, and leaves the toilet seat up. It had certainly done nothing to win her heart so far.

Lt. Fred Frye, USN, wanted children, and he was tired of waiting. If she was really that opposed to having children, he'd said finally, maybe the vision that each of them had of their future together was just too different to be reconciled. Maybe they'd made a huge mistake and they'd better start thinking about how they wanted to deal with that mistake. He had sounded cold and hurt—a strange mix of detached and whiny—like a jet engine shutting down, way in the distance.

And then she touched her tummy and thought about the phone call earlier to Lennie.

"Lennie?"

"Yeah? ... Hi!"

"Hi." Silence.

"What's up?"

"I was wondering something."

"Yeah?"

"Can I come over?"

"Oh. ... Well...I've got, um, company right now."

"Oh." Silence.

"Listen—let me call you—"

"Forget it."

"No! It's just that right now—"

"No, really. It's not that important. Bye."

"Katie—"

Click. She'd hung up.

Bastard, she thought. Sure—okay—she'd been the one to break it off. And sure—every day for the first two of the last three weeks, he'd called the office—the temp agency where she worked—and she'd refused to take his calls. And she'd refused the delivery of the flowers. And then last week she had had Susan at the receptionist's desk tell him when he called that she didn't work there any more—that she'd quit. But still.... *Bastard*, she thought, *the bastard's got another woman over there*. And she was right. And she was wrong.

For six weeks it had been passion. *Real* passion. And danger. The fear of discovery. It had been a forbidden fruit salad. And then he had made the mistake of saying that he was falling in love with her. It wasn't the falling in love. She'd fallen, too. It was the saying of it. The speaking of it out loud. It wasn't something you spoke of when you

109

were gorging yourself on forbidden fruit salad. One doesn't talk with one's mouth full.

Such talk could only lead to a hurt-filled moment of decision. It was scary. It was scarier than the fear of getting caught. It was a different kind of scary. It was sit-down-and-break-someone's-heart scary.

That morning after their first night, he had asked for her telephone number, and she'd given him her number at work and told him he could only call her there—she couldn't...wouldn't...give him her home number...because she was married. And then she was gone.

He called and found out where she worked, and even though he was pretty darn sure it had been a one night thing—one *incredible* night, but one, nonetheless—he sent flowers to her office, anyway. She told them at work that the flowers were from a client—a little "thank you" she told them. Not an absolute falsehood. The card did say "thank you." The full text of the card read: "Wow. Thank you. Call. When you can." Totally monosyllabic. Like much of their night noises had been. And then there was his phone number. She called.

Now she sat on the bed and with one hand on the phone, and the other on her tummy. Beside the phone lay a piece of paper with a phone number that, only now—at that very instant—she knew she would never call again. She rolled the small piece of paper between her thumb and forefinger until it was a tiny, compressed ball, then dropped it into her empty can of Diet Pepsi.

Okay, she thought, *Plan B—let's see, Fred Frye, if you like Daddyville as well you like Bikini-town.*

Chapter 26

The woman was clearly Asian, but she spoke the English of a native Brooklynite. She was talking to the bartender, but Jock Dejohnette sat beside her and listened as if she were speaking only to him.

"I told the super about the leak, like, eighteen times, and I called the landlord twice, and then—boom!—this chunk of my ceiling just collapses. Right into the fucking toilet! If I'd been sitting there, I'd be in the hospital right now. I'd've sued them so quick they wouldn't know what hit 'em."

"There's no justice for the little guy," Jock interjected.

The woman turned and gave him a short jab to the face with her eyes. Jock took it as a barely noticed glancing blow and forged ahead. "All I'm saying is that people who have money and/or power *and* are assholes—and there's an awful lot of them—only seem to notice a response that includes an unignorable threat to their money or power."

"'Un-ig-*nor*-able?' Is that a real word? What're you—a fucking lawyer or something?" the woman asked. "'Cause if you are, I got no money to hire you, and if you're not, what're you sticking your nose in for? To be un-ig-*nor*-able?"

"Like I said—there's no justice," Jock cocked one eyebrow, as if he'd just made some irrefutable point. "I'm a cartoonist. Which, in a way, is *better* than being a lawyer. At least I'm more in the justice business than a lawyer. A lawyer's not in the justice business; he's in the law business." He raised his glass of merlot as if to put a period on his statement.

"A car*toon*ist?" There was more sneer than inquiry in the woman's response. "Don't tell me. You do those sex comics things, right?"

"I draw things the way they *ought* to be. I fix what's wrong with things—with the things that the assholes of the world—like your do-nothing landlord—screw up for the rest of us."

"Yeah? Here—" she slid a bar napkin over toward him "—draw me some justice." When she turned back to her drink, it would have been clear to anyone but Jock that he had been dismissed. With her back to him, she lit a menthol cigarette and returned to that place in her head that sat at the corner of Boredom and Contempt. Jock reached into his pocket for a pen.

By the time she had finished her smoke and turned back to her drink, Jock slid the napkin back to her. She looked at the napkin and cocked her head.

"It's a toilet stuck through the windshield of your landlord's car," Jock said.

"I see. ... I like it." She almost smiled, but stopped herself. "What're you after, anyway? I got a boyfriend, ya know. Italian. Who'd like nothing better than to break your face."

"Oh, yeah?" Jock took another sip of his merlot. "Then why isn't he out breaking your landlord's face?"

"Maybe he is."

"Yeah. Maybe he is. Or maybe he doesn't exist. Except in your head. Like justice. Or on paper, like my cartoons. Whaddayou got—something against talking?"

"No. I got nothing against talking. As long as that's all you're after. You wanna buy me a drink if I gotta listen to you talk?"

"Yeah. I'll buy you a drink."

"And—hey—you're pretty good. With the cartoon thing, I mean."

"It's all yours." He signaled the bartender for another round, then turned back to the woman. "So. You got a name?"

"Yeah, I got a name." She hesitated just long enough to make the average person wonder if she was making it up. "Suzy," she said.

"Well, Suzy—" he said "—who's your favorite superhero?"

"Superhero? Are you serious?"

"Most people go for the ones with some kind of special powers—Superman or Spiderman or one of the X-Men—something like that. I tend to go off the board. I like Zorro."

"Oh, jeez—you *are* fucking serious, aren't you?"

"Goes back to 1919. 'The Curse of Capistrano.' One of those pulp fiction stories. Johnston McCulley—the guy who wrote it—wrote, like, sixty-five of them. Most people just remember

114

the TV show. Guy Williams—remember him? But, ya know, Douglas Fairbanks did the original film version in 1920. Silent."

"Silent," she said. "Silent would be good."

Chapter 27

When Lennie hung up the phone, he lit a cigarette. He walked past Karen Stallings, who sat at one end of his small sofa, her knees drawn up, her chin resting on top of one knee. He opened the french doors of the little bungalow that he called home and stepped out onto the narrow deck that ran around three sides of the place, and just stood there in the moist middle of the Key West night.

"Was that her?" Karen asked.

Lennie took a deep drag and blew the stream of smoke out into the dark before he answered.

"Yeah." That's all he said. There was really nothing else to say. He watched the blinking lights of a jetliner overhead, silently plotting northbound dots in the high emptiness, and for a moment he envied the passengers—whoever they were—it didn't matter—simply because they were going somewhere—anywhere—and they weren't him. *I could change places with any one of them and come out ahead,* he thought.

"Maybe she'll call back," Karen offered from inside.

"Maybe," he said. But somewhere in the cellar of his heart—over in the corner where the enduring sadnesses are stacked—he knew there was a place already cleared for what could've been between him and Katie Frye.

"You want a drink?" Karen asked.

It wasn't a bad idea. He stared out into the

darkness. He pictured one drink leading to another. And another. The two of them—he and Karen— holding each other, each trying to offer the other one some small comfort in this desert-like comfortless stretch of each of their lives. A kiss— more consolation than desire. It had all the makings of rock-a-bye sex between good fuck-buddies. Except they weren't fuck-buddies. He was her boss. And her friend.

"Yeah," he answered, "but just one."

Karen was there at the bungalow because her on-again, off-again boyfriend had run her out of her own apartment. Her married boyfriend. He was drunk, and as he was wont to do when he was in that condition, he had slapped her. Twice. She hadn't waited around for what came next. She had seen it before.

Ordinarily, Lennie would've known how to fix the situation. He would have stopped by and picked up Billy Blackwater, his number two bartender—just for dramatic effect and kickass potential—driven to Karen's place and kicked the sorry son-of-a-bitch to the curb, without a return ticket. But it seemed lately that nothing was simple.

To begin with, the boyfriend—Dennis "The Menace" Chambers—was a cop—one of Key West P.D.'s "finest." Lennie might have gone and kicked his ass out, badge and all, anyway, except he knew that, with Chambers' condition and disposition, someone was liable to get shot in the process, and whoever that turned out to be, he knew, it wouldn't end well for him.

Calling the police would do no good. Karen had called before. A couple of Chambers' buddies would simply show up, spirit him away to one of their places to sober up, and conveniently forget it ever happened. One of them had even told Karen one time, "Hey—you knew what you were getting into when you spread 'em for him the first time. Learn to live with it."

Recently, it had become even more complicated with the Baxter boy incident.

Billy Blackwater was an impressive figure in the bar. He was a most satisfactory bartender, but with built-in optional bouncer features at no extra charge. Billy Blackwater was a full-blooded Seminole. He was tall, well-muscled, and he topped off the picture with an eye-catching Mohawk haircut, just for effect.

Behind the bar, Billy kept a three-foot-long hickory stick, about as big around as a child's baseball bat. The grip end was stippled with hand-carved checkering, above which alternating bands of yellow and crimson paint decorated the shaft. It was the other end, though, that got people's attention. It had been grooved out and fitted with a tomahawk blade—admittedly, a *rubber* tomahawk blade, but dramatic nonetheless. The blade was held in place by leather wrapping strips and was festooned with a feather. Just one. But a controversial one for a while, as it turned out, It was an eagle feather.

The stick hung on a nail behind the bar,

along with a silver referee's whistle on a leather lanyard. Billy Blackwater could quell most disturbances in the bar—not that there were many, but it was, after all, a bar, and thus the site of an occasional eruption—with a blast on the whistle, a taking of the stick in hand, and the admonition: "Don't make me have to come across this bar."

A number of locals had seen the act and would often police their own little outbursts with the only half-joking phrase, "Shhh. Don't make Billy get on the warpath."

The Baxter boy incident was one of those explosions nobody sees coming. He was not a regular, but he had been in a few times. He was only a little more than a year into legal drinking territory.

The night of the incident, he was doing tequila shots and had decided to hit on a female tourist right in front of her husband. Just inside the bar is a sign that reads: *Shirt and shoes required. Bikini tops welcomed and appreciated.* The young woman did a bikini top proud.

The Baxter boy had walked up to the table where the couple sat, leered at the woman's tanned treasures, and said, "Have those puppies been vaccinated?" Before either of them could react, he had leaned over and pressed his face into the top of the puppy on the right, making kissing sounds as he went. When the husband pushed him backwards, the Baxter boy grabbed the long-necked top of one of the Coronas sitting on their table and smashed the bottle against the left side of the husband's head.

119

There was no time for the whistle. Billy Blackwater grabbed the stick and vaulted over the bar. The Baxter boy made the mistake of drawing his arm back, still clutching the broken beer bottle in his fist. The tomahawk chop broke the Baxter boy's right collarbone and sent him to his knees. The follow-up forehand shot smacked directly into his forehead. Everyone agreed later that it was lucky that last shot hadn't fractured his skull. It did, however, put an end to his evening's revelries.

The whole business might have become just one of those things—part temporary minor legal hassle; part long time bar story—except for one detail. The Baxter boy was the son of Hugh Baxter, a city councilman and *not* a big fan of the Key West community of tavern owners to begin with.

Lennie probably could have placated Councilman Baxter and at least mitigated the barrage of harassment he knew was coming, if he had fired Billy Blackwater and thrown him to the wolves. But Lennie wasn't built that way. It just wouldn't have been the right thing to do.

"You need to make a career move," Chambers had told Karen earlier in the evening. She had laughed. That had prompted the first slap. When she called him a bastard and told him to get out, he slapped her the second time, then followed it up with, "Don't be stupid. Stupid pisses me off. Now I'm telling you—you're working at the wrong bar. Got it?"

Karen, Lennie knew, would crash on his

sofa tonight. Nothing would happen. Katie would not call back. Tomorrow, some fine feathered flunky from the fringes of officialdom—building inspector, fire marshal, health inspector, meter maid—would come around and peck him on the ankles.

Lennie remembered when he was a kid, at Easter, he would get a basket stuffed with that shredded green mystery material and topped with a small handful of jellybeans. It wasn't exactly open buffet at Wonka-land, but it always did have a genuine holiday centerpiece: a small hollow milk chocolate bunny. He discovered quickly that the ears and the tail were solid, and he would always begin there—nibbling away at the solid parts, making the whole thing last as long as possible.

Everything around him seemed to be eating away at his solid parts. How long, he wondered, 'til they got down to his hollow center?

Chapter 28

Jock Dejohnette had developed a deep and abiding dislike of dog shit. It wasn't that he was ever fond of it, but it had always been pretty much out of sight, out of mind. As a kid and even as a young adult he had been around dogs—he had even owned a dog once. Briefly. Before it got distemper and his father shot it in the head and buried it in the backyard. And certainly the dogs he had known had gone about the business of doing their business. But it had always been in some out of the way spot—some designated dog shit zone in a back corner of the yard or in some wooded lot. The droppings had always made their way quickly and discreetly into the soil additive category. The most noticeable thing about it, usually, was that the grass was generally greener out there where the dog went. But that was the world of fairly responsible suburban dog-dom, and that dog-dom was worlds apart from the stark realities of dogs in the city. Quite simply, every time Jock came across dog shit on the sidewalks of the city, he sneered in disgust, and his ever-increasing intolerance for those people he considered inconsiderate and stupid dug its sharp claws into his guts. He had seen the people—coming out of their apartments and brownstones—their frantic, urban canines, bladders distended and sphincters clenched, pulling them on their leashes down the steps and up the sidewalks, often only far enough away so that they didn't foul the sidewalk right in front of their own homes. He had seen the people afterwards, urging their dogs to hurry away, leaving the messes for someone else, for everyone else to deal with. The removal system that had evolved seemed to be for inattentive pedestrians to trample through the droppings so that they became smeared enough to dry up and be scuffed away or for the rain to wash away. The only consistent exception seemed to be in the posh neighborhoods of the Upper East Side where dog owners were wealthy enough to hire people to walk their dogs and to clean up after the pets. Jock had decided that as distastefully elitist as it seemed, even to him, dog ownership in the city should be limited to the rich. Most other people, he had decided, were simply too irresponsible, too lazy, or too stupid to be pet owners. He thought that perhaps whoever invented stuffed animal toys may have had that same idea and same target consumer group in mind when he invented fuzzy, huggable, poop-less pooches. But the group hadn't taken the hint. They needed to be taught a lesson, Jock decided. And the Retributor was just the teacher for the job. The thing that finally nudged the problem into the Retributor zone was its intrusion into Jock's lunchtime.

Nellie, of the Pete & Nellie Meat & Deli, knew exactly how much shredded lettuce, exactly how much Gulden's Spicy Mustard, exactly how many paper-thin slices of ham, and exactly how much Swiss cheese Jock liked on his version of ham and cheese on a kaiser roll for lunch. She also knew precisely how crisp the bacon should be and to the nano-dab how much mayonnaise belonged on the perfect BLT. They were the only two items Jock ever ordered when he came into the deli. Twice a week. Tuesdays and Thursdays.

When he came in, Jock liked to make Nellie guess—though it was a severely limited number of sooths from which to choose a say—which it would be, the ham and swiss, or the BLT. Nonetheless, they played the game. Jock would walk up to the counter. Nellie would ask, "What'll it be today?" And Jock would raise his right eyebrow. That was Nellie's signal to guess.

Chapter 29

When Casey Frye graduated in the top 49% of the UVA Class of 1999 and announced that he was going to become a police officer, a lot of people were surprised. They would say things like, "You just don't seem like 'the type,'" which is an interesting concept in itself. That there is "a type"— as if the Justice Department has a clandestine breeding ground somewhere, complete with a secret sperm bank containing samples from J. Edgar Hoover and Melvin Purvis and maybe even Jack Webb, and at which police "types" are carefully and artificially cultivated to form a pool of recruits from which the law enforcement profession fishes for its annual limit.

The interest began the summer before his senior year. He was short one elective, having discovered too late that Music Appreciation had less to do with admiring Janet Jackson's tits or recalling MTV's 100 Sexiest Videos than with recognizing examples of how Beethoven's own mastery of the piano contributed to an extended compass, greater body and richness, and a sustained tone in his compositions for the instrument, or remembering that it was Haydn who developed the string quartet and the sonata forms as they are understood today. To make up the spectacularly failed elective credit hours, he enrolled in an "Introduction to Criminal Justice" class at the nearby community college, and much to his own surprise, really really liked it. He got to know a couple of the officers who were attending there, working on their own degrees, and started doing "ride-alongs" with them. He had been a business major, with no clue where in the business world his little cubicle was waiting, but for the first time he had a picture in his head to attach to such wispy guidance counselor terms as *career opportunity*.

Chapter 30

"Jesus, I hate to miss out on this. Opportunity like this—Christ, who knows when another deal like this'll come along." Taz chewed the end of his cigar and jabbed at the ice cubes in his Diet Coke with a cocktail straw.

"What if it wasn't a full menu operation? Could it be just, like, appetizers, heavy hors d'oeuvres, that kind of thing? Would that qualify?" Woody sipped his drink, knowing already how Taz would respond.

"I don't *want* it to fuckin' *qualify*! If I wanted a fuckin' restaurant, I'd open a fuckin' restaurant. I don't want to put up with the all the shit that you've gotta put up with to run a fuckin' restaurant. Food service is a bitch. A gimme-gimme-gimme, I-love-you-I-hate-you, fuck-me-to-tears bitch. Besides...that location—people aren't comin' in there to eat. They've got nine hundred fuckin' restaurants to choose from already. Another fuckin' restaurant is *not* what that location needs. It needs a *bar*. A nice, classy, we-don't-want-your-baggy-pants-hat-turned-backwards-MTV-hip-hop-ass-*in*-here bar." Taz took his cigar out of his mouth and looked at it like it had gone out on purpose, just to piss him off.

"I'm just asking," Woody shrugged. "Helping you explore the possibilities, as they say."

"Yeah, well, explore the possibilities of this," he grabbed his crotch and shook it a couple of

127

times.

"So buy it up and open a fuckin' bar."

"Not a problem. I *told* you—the problem is fifty thousand, untraceable, well-placed, cash dollars to get a fuckin' liquor license for a brand new bar-only, no-food-service establishment in this fuckin' town. You tell me where to put my hands on that, without pawning my nuts to my brother-in-law's goomba "friends-that-can-help," and I'll dance naked on the bar for you."

Woody thought of the money, vacuum-sealed in plastic, and packed neatly inside the old stereo speakers bolted securely to the bookcase in his apartment...and smiled.

"What?" Taz looked at him. "You?"

"First...promise me you'll stay off the bar," Woody said, as he lit a cigarette and leaned back.

Chapter 31

Dub Zildjian watched the slow-speed police pursuit of O.J.'s white Bronco on the old Sears black and white TV sitting on the table at the front of the garage. *Standard 5.0-liter V8*, he thought, almost automatically. *'Course, rich guy like that prob'ly wasted his money on that optional 5.8.* Dub had replaced the radiator on one recently. An off-road casualty. *Shoot—just not worth it for the maybe six additional horses.*

He lit a generic cigarette and thought about the money. *Either just quit, flat-out, or take a little bit of the money and buy some decent cigarettes,* he thought. He glanced at the back of the garage. An old engine block squatted on a wooden pallet against the back wall. The heavy block reminded Dub more of Jacky Crusoe's tombstone than of the one hundred and seventy-one thousand dollars that had been buried for more than six months in the dirt floor of the garage beneath the big V-8. But the money was beginning to whisper tempting little ideas to him more and more frequently.

Dub was a man at the mercy of his twitches. His hands, his face, his head were in constant motion. You got the impression that if you could somehow physically immobilize him, his nerves would twist and bunch and tie themselves into an actual enormous fibrous knot inside him. His head twisted and bobbed as if trying to prevent the fingers of his right hand from the swift completion of their appointed rounds in touching his right eyelid, his nose, his lower lip, his right ear lobe, the underside of his chin—in an ever-changing sequence not unlike a third-base coach feeding signs to a left-handed batter. Simultaneously, he rapidly twisted his left hand and wrist back and forth like a man trying to jump-start a self-winding watch. His facial expression alternated between wide-eyed astonishment and tight-lipped incredulity—between "That's amazing!" and "Gimme a break." And the two looks seemed in no way to be tied to the other end of whatever snippets of conversation to which the expressions were supposed to be responding. They simply shifted, one counterpoint to the other, then back again, as if on a voice-activated circuit.

His hair was swept back on the sides to form a ducktail at the back of his head. It was a living shrine to Bobby Rydell or maybe Fabian's hair. You were tempted to ask him if he knew the words to "Beach Blanket Bingo," but you were afraid he would actually tell them to you, in a succession of alternately astonished and incredulous line readings.

Chapter 32

Jock Dejohnette was not happy with the way the last civil action had gone. Civil action. That's the term he preferred to apply to the missions that the Retributor undertook. Actions to restore civility to an increasingly *un*-civil society. It wasn't that he was the least sorry or guilt-stricken about the death of the goober tourist who had wrecking-balled his way into the situation. It was simply that this was the first of the civil actions to garner any real attention from the press, and because of the annoying little death of the hayseed, Jock felt that the Retributor and the New York dailies had gotten off on the wrong foot. Jock had envisioned the dailies as allies, of sorts. They were to have been the ones to apply the touches of romantic gilt to the mural depicting the Retributor's exploits. Unfortunately, on the media palette, the midnight blue of the cult hero is soooo close to the asphalt black of the common criminal—the edges of one dollop bleeding into the smear of the other across a muddled no-man's-land of nameless smudge—that the slightest mis-daub of the press' brush tip can wrongly tinge a character almost indelibly. Ask any superhero you happen to see—the mask and hood of the righteous are heavier than they look. One other note for those seeking a "lovable outlaw" image with a slice of the "admiring public" pie on the side: shooting a dog will cut seriously into your fan base.

It had begun on the Thursday before Labor

Day. Jock was sitting alone at a small table by the window and had just begun to enjoy his ham and Swiss on a kaiser roll—a selection which Nellie had divined correctly and constructed perfectly. Jock liked the table; in truth, he thought of it as "his" table, and he was always a bit cross when he came in and discovered someone else occupying "his" table. Part of the attraction of the table was the view it afforded of a second story apartment above a dry cleaners directly across the street from the Pete & Nellie Meat & Deli establishment. The resident of the apartment was a young lady with a casual attitude toward nudity as she padded around her place and a matching casual attitude toward the necessity of window blinds. She was a redhead, early thirties, Jock figured, with a few extra pounds. Jock liked to imagine that she knew he was watching—that it was part of a very secret, sensuous game they were playing. And today, "his" table was all his. She was in the bathroom—the one room in the apartment where the window was frosted. Still, he could see her blurred flesh-colored form moving about inside. It must have been like every trip Mr. Magoo ever made to a titty bar. For Jock, it was exactly the teasing touch he liked at the beginning of their little private game. It whetted all of his appetites, and he chewed slowly and steadily into his sandwich.

The man—Shane Callahan—was an habitual gambler. Under other circumstances he would have appreciated the odds involved in his choosing that precise moment to walk up and block Jock's view of the blurry burlesque. But Shane Callahan was also a chronically unlucky gambler. The reason for his pause there on the sidewalk just on the other side of the plate glass window from where Jock sat was that Duchess, his big brindle boxer dog, had chosen that exact time and place to squat and discharge the disagreeable load in her bowels. The night before, Shane Callahan had come across what had once been half of a chicken in his refrigerator, and he had dumped it into the trash can in the corner of his kitchen. He had awoken very late that morning to the rank realization that Duchess had spent the morning gorging herself on the contents of that trash can. And now, finally—on the sidewalk in front of the Pete & Nellie Meat & Deli—the fetid fowl was flying the coop in almost the exact color and consistency of the Gulden's mustard that graced the ham and Swiss in Jock's hands. Jock gagged. When Duchess straightened up, Shane gave a gentle tug on her leash, and the two of them strode away with the proud gait of ones making an entrance into the arena of the Westminster Dog Show.

Chapter 33

Though Becky Bedecky would never know it, had Jacky Crusoe lived long enough to get caught—and there was no doubt in Dub's mind that, eventually, Jacky *would* have been caught—he would have dragged Becky into the whole mess right up to her mischievous blue eyes. Jacky had said more than a couple of times that it was basically Becky's idea—a notion she would have squealed in protest of. She was a squealer. Squealing was her emotional outburst of choice.

She referred often to the four and a half years she had spent at Wachovia Bank. It was a ready frame of reference for her observations on everything from the perils of workplace romances to the glaringly inadequate security measures she observed at her present job in the business office at Charlotte Motor Speedway. It was her repeated assertion that the racetrack management was just *asking* for someone to walk off with their money that had first planted the idea in Jacky's head. "It's like she thinks it would serve them right," Jacky had offered.

Jacky Crusoe was a dirt-track racer on the weekends; Becky Bedecky was a racing fan. Jacky and Becky dated for five months before the plan gelled in Jacky's mind. By that time he had lost count of the number of times she had walked him through the counting and securing of the speedway's money—complete with each security flaw along the way. The "vault"—little more than a storage closet—was the most vulnerable and the least risky spot for the "taking-candy-from-a-baby" deed. She would hold up her keys and say, "Every time I hand these to that sorry excuse for a security guard, and he opens the door, I expect somebody to be waiting there to stick a gun right in our faces." But armed robbery was not Jacky's style. Too many things could go wrong when there was a gun involved. But those keys jingle-jangled in his head until the plan came together.

Getting the keys and having copies made was easy. By that time, he was a familiar face, not just around the racetrack—after all, he had been around there for years—but in the business office area, where he made it a point to become a frequent visitor—stopping by early to wait for Becky to get off work or presenting her with flowers for her desk while basking in the "Oooo's" and "Ahhh's" from Becky's female co-workers.

"Casing the joint." Jacky liked the Bogey-esque sound of it. After he'd had the duplicate keys made, he would slip away, under pretense of visiting the restroom, and let himself into the room where the "vault" kept its pitiful watch over office supplies and old receipts until race days. It was during one of these "bathroom breaks" that Jacky first familiarized himself with the crawl-space inside the air conditioning return. It was a fairly easy fit. The trick, he had decided, would be to develop the necessary patience. Lots of patience.

He found a cardboard box that approximated the crawl space, and as race day approached, Jacky began to spend hours in the box. "In training" is how he thought of it.

When the roar of race day finally filled the air, it was almost too easy. *Becky was right—it's like they were just asking for it*, he thought. A hundred and eighty-six thousand. Just like that. A couple of hours of cramped quarters, a turn of the key, and a casual stroll from the office section through the tunnel to the pits area, and—bingo!—a hundred and eighty-six thousand dollars. Why couldn't everything in life be so simple?

Becky was absolutely in the clear. She was present in the office, except for her trip with the security guard to the "vault room," on their first trip. She was with the security guard again on the second trip, when the theft was discovered. She squealed.

A week later, Jacky took a trip to Las Vegas. He lost a lot of money. He was a pretty high-profile loser. Since he was a "cash player," nobody was sure exactly how much he dropped. Nobody except Jacky. Fifteen thousand dollars. The remainder— one hundred and seventy-one thousand—was nestled into a hole beneath a V-8 engine at the back of Dub's garage. It was supposed to be the seed money that was to move the racing team of Crusoe and Zildjian from the dirt tracks of Gaffney, South Carolina and Bristol, Tennessee to the NASCAR circuit, eventually. It was a long shot; but like Jacky liked to say, "A long shot is *still* a shot." They had it all planned out. And then Jacky took out a section of wall in the fourth turn of the Dixie Speedway, and didn't walk away. Ever again. So Dub smoked generic cigarettes and listened to the whisper of the hundred and seventy-one thousand dollars from beneath the engine block at the rear of his garage. Sometimes he wished it would just disappear.

Chapter 34

"Just promise me we won't name it Strike Three," Woody said. He was to be a full-fledged partner now with Tony and Taz in what would be the third location. Tony couldn't be there today; he was busy at the Strike One, and he'd told them whatever they came up with would be fine. They just needed a name to go on the new liquor license.

"What's wrong with Strike Three?" Taz asked.

Woody raised his eyebrows and looked at him. "Think about it. Think about the implications. Think of the ominous connotations of the name in terms of a business venture."

Taz chewed his cigar a moment, set his jaw, and locked his eyes on something faraway in what Woody could only assume was Taz' "think mode." After a few moments, he shook himself out of his trace and said, "Oh. Yeah. ... So what'll we name it? You got ideas?"

It's interesting—the varying degrees of importance one puts on a name, Woody thought. He remembered Lorna—Lorna Devondeffer River, actually—a porcelain doll of a woman with a full, sensuous mouth and eyes you could free fall into like a sky diver, whom he had met during the first few weeks after he had begun to frequent the Strike Two.

During their third drink, she began to tell him about the parade of losers that in recent months had goose-stepped their way through her dating life. The bad toupees. The sleezeballs who suffered from SSO syndrome—Sudden Significant Other syndrome—who after about the third date remembered suddenly that they had a wife or a girlfriend or in one case a *boy*friend. The poet who, ten minutes into their first drink, pulled out his recently deceased wife's obituary which he had penned and published in the newspaper, and offered her a poetic reading of it. The body builder who, fifteen minutes into their salad appetizers, proudly announced that he was the recent recipient of a modern marvel of erectile engineering—an implanted penis pump—and said that he would be proud to have her give it its first test drive and help him put it through its paces.

During her fifth Ketel One martini, she confessed that Lorna Devondeffer River was not her birth name—that she had changed it from Debbie Daniel. He started to tell her that she really *looked* more like a Debbie than a Lorna, but thought better of it. For a moment, he even toyed with the idea of telling her how much they suddenly had in common, but then he put that toy back on the shelf.

As kind of a last ditch effort to figure out the reason behind her string of romantic failures, she told him, a friend referred her to a seer and palm reader who referred to herself as an "anagrammatical psychologist." A basic premise of anagrammatical psychology is that oftentimes our relationships with other people are shaped by the anagrams that others make from our name—usually not consciously, of course, but as part of the subconscious analytical undertakings that we all engage in as we try to make sense of the world around us and make choices in life. The more reassuring or attractive the anagrams our subconscious comes up with from someone's name, the more we are drawn to that person; the more troubling the anagrams, the more likely we are to flee the relationship. The analysis was quick, painless, and left no doubt as to her next course of action. She rambled through her purse, found her wallet, and withdrew a folded copy of the report she got from the anagramological advisor. Woody wasn't sure whose word that was— anagramological—hers or the "advisor's" or the Ketel One's.

NAME: Debbie Daniel
INITIAL SCAN RESULTS:

Subconscious Anagram	Subconscious Tag
1. I need a dibble.	1. Cutesy
2. Be in ideal bed.	2. Confucian
3. I'd need a bible.	3. Evangelical
4. Edible in a bed.	4. Sensuous
5. Deb need alibi.	5. Disturbing
6. I blinded a bee.	6. Maniacal
7. I bleed in a bed.	7. Creepy

As soon as she saw the progression—or declension, rather—of the accompanying tags, her mind was made up. She would change her name. The only question was: *what would be her new name*? Recommendations, she discovered, were available...for a fee.

The name she decided on was Lorna Devondeffer River, which anagrammed out to "friend and lover forever." She always introduced herself using the complete name, though it did sound a little pretentious, even to her, unwilling to risk whatever saboteur anagrams might be lurking beneath the surface of the simple Lorna River.

After the sixth drink, they took the conversation to Woody's place, where they tried out the "friend and lover" part, but made a shambles of the overly optimistic "forever" qualifier.

Some time later, Woody, during a moment of idle curiosity, took an anagrammatical stab at Woody Zildjian on a bar napkin, but as soon as "zany dildo" began to take shape, he stopped, wadded up the napkin, and threw it away.

"How 'bout *Ball One*?" Taz suggested.

"Ball one?"

"Yeah. You know, like, strike one...strike two...*ball one*. Kinda keeps it in the spirit of things, but no strike three. Ya know? Plus, it leaves room for growth. Ball Two, Ball Three...."

"Why not?" Woody sighed.

"All right," Taz smiled, obviously pleased with himself, "Ball One it is."

Chapter 35

Absolutely untraceable. That's the way Jock Dejohnette thought of the Savage Model 1907 .32-caliber pistol that fit so comfortably in his hand. He had come across it several years back in a box in his father's closet when his mother asked him to go through his father's things after the old man died. In the box with the pistol was a folded advertisement featuring a picture of a bow-tied Bat Masterson, looking more like Peter Lorre in *The Maltese Falcon* than a wild West gunslinger. The caption read: *"Bat" Masterson Says: "A tenderfoot with a Savage Automatic and the nerve to stand his ground, could have run the worst six-shooter man, the West ever knew, right off the range."* If the Savage Automatic was good enough for Bat Masterson, Jock thought, it was just perfect for the Retributor.

In Issue #3, the Retributor rescues the great-granddaughter of Bat Masterson from a gang of young thugs, and to show her appreciation, the young woman makes a gift of her great-grandfather's own personal Savage .32 Automatic Model 1907 to the Retributor. In the last few frames, she plants a kiss on Retributor's rugged cheek and says, "Grandpa Bat did his best to clean up the old West. Maybe this'll help you clean up the west *side*." Jock red-inked the lipstick trace on the Retributor's cheek.

Guns, of course, don't have a soul by which

to be judged; they only have a history. If its history is remarkably noble or remarkably infamous, the gun ends up not in heaven or hell, but in a museum. The bland history of most, though, condemns them to walk the earth in the pockets and waistbands of people as bland as themselves or to haunt the top shelves of closets filled with the rag-tag remnants of lackluster lives. If the thing were a finely crafted violin socked away in the back of a closet, doomed never to sing the notes for which it was created, we would think, *how sad!* But such tender sensibilities are not to be afforded to the blued steel thing left to worry itself to rust under the weight of its desuetude. One wonders if, after years and years of such solitary neglect, a particularly sensitive sidearm might not become a bit overanxious to speak its mind. That's the way it felt to Jock Dejohnette when the Retributor went to set things right with Shane Callahan and Duchess—like the Savage .32 Automatic just "went off"…almost on its own.

Chapter 36

For six months after Jacky Crusoe's fatal crash at the Dixie Speedway, Dub Zildjian's already herky-jerky nervous system shifted into four-wheel drive and went off-roading. He had dreams in which he inexplicably found himself onstage at the Grand Ole Opry, clutching the old duffle bag of money in his arms. Ryman Auditorium was filled to the rafters with everyone he had ever met in his life. Down front were his mother and father, his grandparents, the preacher from the church that he had attended as a boy, his high school principal, and Billy Graham. Onstage, surrounding him, were Bill Monroe, Roy Acuff, Grandpa Jones, Hank Williams—Sr. *and* Jr., Lester Flatt and Earl Scruggs, The Wilburn Brothers—Teddy and Doyle, Porter Wagoner, Carl Perkins, and Elvis. They were singing an almost raucous slightly up-tempo bluegrass rendition of "Just a Closer Walk with Thee." Beside him, his great-uncle Gene—his grandfather's brother—sat in his wheelchair and kept reaching into the duffle bag and pulling out handfuls of cash, while Dub struggled to retrieve the money and stuff it back into the bag without everyone seeing it. The more frantic the struggle became between Dub and his uncle Gene, the faster the tempo of the song became and the louder the group sang. As thousands of bills began to spill out all over the stage, the volume swelled and the tempo raced and the audience joined in the frenzied clamor of the hymn. And then he would jerk upright in bed, awake, and sweating, and he would light up a generic cigarette and wait for the ringing of the hymn to leave his head.

Not one to delve too deeply into dream analysis, Dub, nonetheless, knew anxiety when it bit him in the face, and knew he had to do *something* with the hidden cash. He also knew he had to find a better way of coping with the anxiety until he figured out what that *something* was. Had his great-uncle Gene not shown up with such regularity and prominence in the dream, Dub probably would not have sought solace in the soothing succor of Southern Comfort. At the Zen Den.

The tale of how Great-uncle Gene ended up in a wheelchair had served as a highly effective evils-of-alcohol cautionary tale for Dub his whole life. In the company of Jacky Crusoe, he would eventually sip a glass of beer, which he repeatedly and liberally sprinkled with salt, but that was the extent of his careful forays into the Land of the Demon Alcohol. Both of his parents had been teetotalers. In fact, most everyone in his family that he knew abstained. Or indulged in such secret moderation that they could sit beside the teetotalers at a revival meeting and hardly break a sweat. And this was all because of Uncle Gene.

Uncle Gene suffered from what they called Jake Leg—a numbness, weakness, tingling sensation in the legs, often leading to paralysis. Permanent. It came from drinking Jamaican ginger extract—a concoction that was 85% alcohol, but cut with a chemical called TOCP—triorthosylphosphate. That was the culprit. Though alcohol took the rap for it.

During Prohibition, Uncle Gene developed a taste for the stuff. About 1932, the stuff apparently developed a taste for him. It pretty much ate up his lower spine, apparently, and Uncle Gene became one of about 50,000 or so jake-leggers. It was enough to give a man the blues.

> *I can't eat*
> *I can't talk*
> *Been drinkin' mean jake, lord*
> *Now I can't walk.*
> *Ain't got nothin' now*
> *Left to lose*
> *'Cause I'm a jake-walkin' papa*
> *With the jake leg blues.*

Uncle Gene knew all the words to all the verses. Because he'd heard Dub's grandfather sing it. A thousand times.

And so Uncle Gene became the family's very own poster-boy-on-wheels for just what drinking could reduce a man to. Grandpa Zildjian made sure that Uncle Gene was wheeled in for every family gathering, and he would make sure that Uncle Gene's glass of iced tea was always full. It seemed like he was just waiting for Uncle Gene to finally say he had to go the bathroom, so that he could say, "'S just a shame, ain't it, what liquor'll do? There ain't nothin' sadder than a grown man who can't even stand up to make his water."

Just once, Dub would have liked to have seen Uncle Gene stand up and tell them all to kiss his rusty butt and just walk away. Sometimes he wished *he* could just walk away.

In the original draft of the plan, the Retributor, in the guise of a sanitation worker would spend the day at the Prospect Park dog park, scooping up puppy poop and depositing it into a five-gallon plastic bucket. He would carry the bucket to the brownstone residence of Shane Callahan and Duchess, where he would use a glass cutter to remove a hole near the top of the glass panel in the storm door. Into that portal he would trowel the entire contents of the collected dog droppings until it filled the space between the storm door and the front door, creating a virtual wall of dog shit that would collapse in the face of the unsuspecting Mr. Callahan when he opened his front door to take the Duchess out for her morning deposit. But then, Jock began to do the math.

Figuring the door to be 30 inches wide, and the space between the storm door and the front entryway door to be four inches, to fill the gap to a height of five feet meant packing in 7200 cubic inches of canine crap. Considering that one gallon contains 231 cubic inches, he realized he was looking at collecting and transporting over 30 gallons of the stuff. 260-plus pounds of pooch poo. And while he had complete confidence in the fecal-generating potential of Brooklyn's bowwows, even the most dedicated seeker of justice, he thought, shouldn't have to put up with that much shit. Thus was born Plan B.

Chapter 38

A man can be lured away from the last ten minutes of a tie-scored Super Bowl game by the right sexual enticement. That is because Sex is *the* trump card. It is a sure bet that the phrase "better than sex" was coined by a woman. That is because there *is* at least a short list of things that, for women, are better than sex. For men, the phrase "better than sex" is as nonsensical as "scooter my daisy head."[1] Try to initiate sex with a woman who is one bite into a dessert called "Death By Chocolate," and you are liable to wind up with a dessert fork stuck in your eye. Countless men have switched off World Series games for the sake of sex, never even suspecting that the sex was offered for no other reason *than* sport—to get those men to switch off a World Series game! Never in history, though, has a woman walked away in mid-pedicure to go have sex. What women do not seem to realize is the cruelty of suggesting—true or not—that there is something better than sex. Telling a man that something is better than sex is like giving a seven-year-old Santa's head in a box with a bow on Christmas morning.

Merilee snuggled up to Woody and molded herself to his side. For a few minutes, they just enjoyed the feeling of warm skin against warm skin—lying there in their matching ionogenic body stockings, playing buzz-o-riffic games up and down the sidelines of each other's force field.

"Why the bar business?" she asked.

"I like bars," he answered.

"I like sex, but I'm not opening a brothel," she smiled. Her fingertips brushstroked his chest.

"Snappy. You had your reparteé re-strung yesterday, didn't you?" he smiled back.

"Ever been in the bar business before?"

"I've sorta run...a couple...of places." He accented the pauses with brushstrokes of his own across her left nipple, then her right.

"Oh, yeah? Where?"

"Oh...here and there." His hand caressed the undercurve of each breast.

"When it comes to the past, you don't give a girl much to go on, do you?"

"More interested in keeping her pleasantly distracted in the present." His hand slid lower, over the smooth skin of her tummy.

"But what's a girl to think?" She made a playfully pouty face.

He put on a mock-serious face. "You're to think anything you'd like. It's *your* brain; you mustn't ever let anybody tell you what or how to think. And asking is just an invitation for some people to tell you exactly that."

"Stop it. You know what I mean." She poked him in the side.

He sighed. "Is this where we tell each other our life stories?"

"Well, not our whole *life stories*...."

"Oooo, I wish I'd known. Unfortunately, a

150

couple of years ago, I made a deal with that part of my brain that really loves college football and John Wayne movies and the Three Stooges that if it would sneak up on that part of the brain that compels us to tell other people our life stories and smother it in its sleep that I would never make it sit through an entire ballet for the rest of my life, sooooo..."

"Very funny."

"Oh. I meant to ask you. You don't pirouette or jeté, do you?"

"Welllll..." her voice shifted into a sultrier register, "what if I told you I had a sort of...history fetish? That I find details of a man's past *very* sexually stimulating?" Her hand slipped lower across his belly until, just as it reached his bellybutton, it grazed the tip of his erect penis, rising to meet her halfway.

"I'd say...I was born at 2:22 a.m. on a very hot night in August. There had been quite a dry spell for several weeks prior to my birth, but on that very night, a thunderstorm moved in. My parents were poor, but honest, working folks who brought me home from the hospital in an old '32 Mercury that was the first car my dad ever owned. He bought it second-hand from a man named Griff whom he'd known since grammar school. ... How'm I doin' so far?" Her hand closed around the trunk of his cock and squeezed.

"Oh, I'd say we were getting there," she whispered, as she moved on top of him.

Chapter 39

When Ray Black sat back and observed Dub Zildjian, as he so often did with his customers at the Zen Den, he supposed that Dub suffered from some nerve disorder—not a nervous condition—something of the physiological ilk, something along the line of Parkinson's, perhaps. But the more he watched him, the more he noticed the pattern of Dub's movements, the tic-like quality of the twitches—and he began to wonder just what it was that plagued the man and jabbed him so unrelentingly with its invisible little pitchforks. Even without the twitch show, Dub would have looked out of place in the Zen Den. But he was always there with Jacky Crusoe, and Ray just figured he was one of Jacky's hangers-on, maybe even a relative that Jacky kept around him out of pity or as a curiosity piece. Jacky was right in his element at the bar. Though Jacky, too, would not have fit in with most of the folks who frequented the bar in their lives outside the bar, he had just the right dusting of bad boy charm—racecar driver, renegade, good-time Charlie—that he was never at a loss for companionship. If he wasn't flirting with one, or sometimes even two, of the female customers, he had a table full of nine-to-five guys steeped neck-deep in the vicarious testosterone soup of some 160 mph adventure that he was holding forth on. His companion, Dub, though, was something of a puzzlement. He stayed in the background and seemed to like to watch. But not with the starry eyes of a hero-worshiper. It was more like someone who had baited a field with corn to attract exotic wildlife, not so that he could shoot them, but just so he could watch them as they fed and preened and moved about in their otherwise unseen exotic lives.

When Jacky Crusoe spun-out and crashed through the southeast wall around this vale of tears, people at the Zen Den were surprised, though they were not what you would call shocked and saddened. It was as if this was another of Jacky's stunts, and at any moment, Jacky would come bopping into the bar, pull a chair up to a group of guys at a table, nudge one of them with his elbow and say, "Hey, is that your wife comin' in?" and when the guy looked, reach over and steal his drink, then say, "Oh, hey—jeez—did you hear about me gettin' killed at Dixie? You're not gonna believe how that happened. Lemme tell you—." It was like he was an act that had closed—the Jacky Crusoe Show!—and had moved on to some other venue. A lot of folks were glad they had caught the act while it was in town, but they didn't give a lot of thought as to where it might be playing now. And they certainly didn't give any thought to the odd twitchy guy in the back row of the chorus. It wasn't until some months after the crash when Dub showed up that first time alone—on his own; Jacky-less—that Ray even realized that he hadn't seen him and hadn't really even thought about him.

But now he was kind of curious. They began to talk. With time and the introduction of Southern Comfort into their little circle, Dub Zildjian had a story to tell that was every bit as remarkable as his repertoire of twitches.

Dub Zildjian didn't come to the Zen Den to seek enlightenment. He wasn't even sure what zen *was*, though he thought it might have something to do with kung fu, and he *had* liked the TV show. Besides, Jacky had liked the place, so it and the guy who ran it must be okay, he figured.

There had not been a lot of intellectual conversations in Dub's life. There had been even fewer life-changing ones.

The first one that came to mind occurred when he was thirteen and his momma had decided it was time for him to talk to the preacher, Reverend McIntyre, about joining the Corinth Baptist Church.

"I just have one question to ask you, son," Reverend McIntyre had said to him. "Do you love Jesus?"

"I love Jesus," Dub had answered.

"Praise the Lord," the reverend had said, "let's git 'er done!"

The second occasion was when he had met with a high school guidance counselor, who had looked at Dub's scholarly efforts up to that point and was suggesting that Dub consider shifting from the standard academic track to the vocational training track.

"Do you like cars, son?" the guidance

154

counselor had asked him.

"I love cars," Dub had answered.

"Well, there you go," the counselor had said, "let's get you swapped over then!"

That night at the Zen Den, as Dub sipped the sweet nectar of the Southern Comfort, he found himself nearly mesmerized by the calm voice of Ray Black, who sat beside him, nursing a rum and Coke, and talked to him like no one had ever talked to him before.

"At some point you have to decide what's more important—being who you are—I don't mean being the name someone typed on your birth certificate or the person your mother or father or someone else always wanted you to be—I mean *who you are*. Or—being the lifelong caretaker of all the *stuff* that has attached itself to the existence you've been tending according to someone else's expectations. If all the material trappings are more important, then learn to love that particular pretense of who you call *self*. Just go with it as long as the stuff lasts. But...if you choose to be *you*—once you really make that choice—you just shake off all that stuff, like a dog emerging from a creek and shaking off water. All of it. Your car. Your old high school yearbook. The entire contents of your junk drawer in the kitchen. Your checkbook. Your unopened telephone bill. That name on your driver's license. All of it. You walk away. Be who you are. The stuff that goes along with who you are will just naturally adhere itself to you as you go. Then...if

155

you wake up one day—or *when* you wake up one day and realize you're not who you used to be—or who you used to *think* you were—you shake it off again and just keep going."

"The name on your driver's license?" Dub's eyes shifted into astonished mode.

"Yeah, I know. The way the world is set up, you really have to have a name of some sort for who you think you really are. So you get another name—one that you're not so attached to, like you were to the old one. Once you know who you *are*...it doesn't really matter what you call yourself."

"I had a pair of work boots that I wore for nine years. Got 'em re-soled 'til there was almost nothin' left to re-sole. Then I duct-taped 'em."

"But eventually...you had to get some new ones, right?"

"Yeah."

"Yeah."

"I kept 'em, though. They're in a bag in my closet. All mildewed, last time I looked at 'em."

"That's what stuff'll do to you—if you choose stuff—make you watch it turn to shit and take you right along with it. Becomes a matter of—do you have it, or does it have you?"

Dub looked intently at Ray Black, trying to focus, then jumped a little, as if he had bumped a live wire with his left shoulder. He touched his right ear, his chin, and his lips with the fingertips of his right hand, three times in quick succession, then craned his neck hard to the right. His eyes grew wide, then narrowed, and he leaned forward toward Ray.

"I'm gonna tell you something. It's about...like what you're talkin' about—stuff. I never told nobody about it."

"You know what? At this point, I'd rather you didn't. It's not that I don't want to hear. I'm just afraid it would be the Southern Comfort talking right now."

"Oh," Dub looked at his glass and jerked as if it had somehow startled him. He picked it up, took a sip, and said, "I love this stuff."

"Tell you what—why don't you sleep on it. If you still want to talk about it tomorrow, come on back. You can tell it over the first drink, instead of the...whichever one that is tonight."

Nobody talked to Dub. *Really* talked. They just couldn't seem to get past the twitches and facial expression shifts. Nobody except Jacky, that is. Or was.

People did speak to him—to describe the noise their car was making, or to see if they could bring the car in on a Sunday, but nobody really conversed with him. Even the Jehovah's Witnesses usually just handed him a *Watchtower* and left.

Ray Black didn't seem to be bothered by the herky-jerky pattern of Dub's dance around Life's communal campfire. It was like trying to read a Kerouac novel through an electric fan. Most people couldn't get beyond the blades flashing around in front of them. But if you looked through all the commotion, there was a helluva road trip in there somewhere. Ray Black had already caught a glimpse of Dub's luggage, packed and ready, just beyond the flickering facade.

When Dub Zildjian *became* Donald Rayfield Black, the name Ray had already been taken by his predecessor, and the name Don had already been taken by his predecessor's predecessor—the original Donald Rayfield Black. Dub Zildjian's creative gene was recessive to the point of regressive. And thus Dub Zildjian would become Blackie Black.

If anyone had ever asked Dub Zildjian *or* Blackie Black—though nobody ever had—if he would like to go to New York City, his answer likely would have been along the lines of he wouldn't be caught dead there. But, oddly enough, he was.

When Woody Zildjian read in the *New York Post* the account of the bizarre death of Blackie Black, he remarked to his bowl of Rice Crispies that it was, indeed, a strange, strange world that we lived in. His cereal snapped, crackled, and popped in enthusiastic agreement.

Chapter 40

"I found him. I think."

"What? Who? Lennie Lupo?"

"Yeah. I think so. I found the bar, at least."

"Lupo's? It's still there?"

"Yeah. Apparently it's almost an institution now in Key West."

"Oh, my God, Casey. How did you find it?"

"Simple. The internet. You can find anything."

"Does he have a website? Pictures?"

"No. At least none that I've found."

"Did you call?"

"No."

"No?"

"I'm going there, Mom."

"You're going...? Do you want me... I mean, if you want..."

"No. I'm going alone. But I do need your help with one thing."

"Of course. Money? I can—"

"Not money. ... Well...maybe money. Later. But that's not the main thing right now."

"Oh. ... What, then?"

"You remember Rick Carney? Nick's older brother?"

"Yes, of course."

"He's a detective now, you know. Norfolk P.D."

"Oh. And...?"

"What I was wondering was.... I mean, I sorta figured that you didn't have a picture or anything of this guy."

"No. I don't."

"Well, they have this computer program—Norfolk, I mean; we don't have the budget for something like that—where you can describe someone, and they can put together a picture of someone."

"Like a sketch artist."

"Yeah. But you don't have to be an artist. You just have to know how to use the program. Anyway...I talked to Rick, and if you'd be willing to sit down with him, he thinks he might be able to put together a picture."

"Casey...it would be a picture of how he looked twenty-three years ago."

"Yeah. I thought of that. There are other programs, though—if I could find one—that can, like, age a picture of someone. You know—how they'd look now. I don't know. It's a starting point."

She paused and looked at him.

"You want a starting point? A picture of how he looked...twenty-three years ago?

"I thought you said you didn't—"

From her purse she withdrew a compact and flipped it open. She turned the mirror to Casey's face. "Take a good look."

Casey looked at himself in the mirror for a moment, then looked at his mother. "That has to have been pretty weird for you, huh?"

"Weird doesn't begin to cover it."

"I, uh, wanted to tell you something, Mom."

"What is it, baby?"

"About Dad. I...I didn't tell him. I just figured it would be best if...."

"If...I told him?"

"...Or not. It's up to you. ... I mean, with him just getting married again and all...."

"Yeah. I'm not sure Emily Post covers the appropriate time to drop those kinds of bombs on newlyweds."

"At least maybe he'll be relieved about the operation. About his part, I mean."

"He'll feel bad for *you*. He really would do anything for you, you know."

"I know."

"I suspect his new young bride will be more relieved than he'll be. ... Oooo. Was that as catty as I think it was?"

"Maybe a little."

"So when are you going to Florida?"

"I'm looking for a good price on a flight now. The clock is tickin', you know."

"Oh, my God, Casey. You mean you're going to ask him about the operation?"

"Why'd you *think* I was going to find him—to wish him a Happy Father's Day?"

"Have you thought about what you're going to say to him?"

"Not exactly. ... But I haven't ruled out: 'Did you ever think to yourself, *I'd give my left nut to*

Chapter 41

Blackie Black had worked at Hirie's Exxon station since the third day he had arrived in Myrtle Beach in 1994. He had made a deal with himself that, as much as he'd always wanted to live at the beach, he wouldn't allow himself to even see the ocean until he'd gotten a job. The story he had come up with to fill in the blanks of his past was that, for the last several years, he'd been traveling with carnies. No permanent addresses to come up with. No personal references. It was the kind of life that didn't ink out the job applications of big companies like Sears or K-Mart very well. Hirie Meeks, on the other hand, wasn't offering paid vacations or health insurance or profit-sharing retirement plans, and his last mechanic had left him a note—"Gone to work for Big Dawg Charters"—stuck to the front door of the service station with a piece of black electrical tape. Even so, when he first met Blackie Black, Hirie immediately thought of the line—"itchin' like a man on a fuzzy tree"—from the old Elvis song, and then the song was stuck in his head, and he couldn't remember the rest of the words. While the tune rambled around in his head, he asked Blackie a few questions, watched him do a rear brake job on a minivan, and finally told Blackie he would give him a try. Seven years later, the "fuzzy tree" line still popped into Hirie's head on a fairly regular basis when watched Blackie for any time at all, but he would tell anyone that, if he had to get work done on his own mother's car, he wouldn't take it to anybody but Blackie. Hirie wasn't the type to ask a lot of personal questions, and Hirie's lack of questions was a perfect fit for Blackie's lack of answers.

And then there was Hirie's wife, Mimi—a woman with a centerfold's body and a startlingly ugly face. As folks said behind her and Hirie's back—a body that would stop traffic and a face that would stop a clock. She was also a bit on the simple-minded side, and she was as fascinated with Blackie's shakes and twitches as he was with the extraordinary incongruity of her figure and her face. Whenever she came to the station the two of them spent an awful lot of time staring at each other with amused grins on their faces, as if neither could see the other's undisguised fascination. And they called each other Mr. Black and Missus Meeks. Blackie was especially fond of the jars of homemade olives stuffed with garlic cloves that she brought by the station. For the last few years, whenever she brought a jar to the station, she brought an extra jar for Blackie to take home with him.

Certainly, there were times when Blackie questioned whether he'd made the right decision about the money. The one hundred and seventy-one thousand dollars. But deep down, he knew that, if he had kept it or spent it opening up a new garage in a new place, someone somewhere would've asked the wrong question at the right time or the right question at the wrong time, and he would've ended up in jail. He had always felt most at ease with a wrench in his hand. Mechanical solutions to mechanical problems, that's what he liked. All the years he spent hanging out with Jacky Crusoe, it was always Jacky who'd had all the answers. It was Jacky who'd done the talking. It was Jacky who was comfortable telling the jokes, flirting with the women, taking off to places like Las Vegas. It was Jacky who liked to hang out at the Zen Den bar in Charlotte. It was at the Zen Den that Dub Zildjian had met Ray Black. It was at the Zen Den that Ray Black and Dub Zildjian had sat down with their false notions of identity and had finessed the details of the exchange that had led them to the who's that each of them now was. Woody—for he had decided on Woody almost immediately—as it turned out, had to have the length of his new false notion let out just a little. Blackie—happy with the moniker that took him back to the *Boston Blackie* Saturday nights of his early childhood—didn't mind the rumpled look at all.

Chapter 42

With all due respect to Brother John Lennon—instant karma is probably *not* gonna getcha. The *quest* for instant karma, however, just might. Because karma is too big to fit in a vacuum-sealed, freshness-guaranteed foil insta-pack. It is too big to fit in your grandfather's clock that was too large for the shelf so it stood ninety years on the floor. It barely fits in God's watchpocket. In terms of a sense of schedule, it is the Great Cosmic Tom Cat in the Great Scheme of Things. It comes and goes as it pleases. You can put out saucer after saucer of the milk of human kindness; you can fill your back porch with Purina Karma Chow; but it will show up when, and *only* when, it's good and damned ready. Just when you've decided that it must've been run over and flattened by the Starland steamroller and it's never coming home, you may open the back door and there it is—figure-eighting through your legs and covering your trouser legs with cosmic cat hair. Or...it may lie nonchalantly beneath the next door neighbor's badly dinged Buick and lazily groom itself, and leave you standing for a lifetime on your back porch calling, "Here, kitty, kitty, kitty...." You just never know.

"Lennie Lupo?"

From behind the counter, Larry turned and looked at the figure silhouetted in the wide doorway of the bar. The pre-noon Florida sun blindingly back-lighted the man. The silhouette didn't appear to Larry to belong to a man who was old enough or shabby enough to be a morning drinker. *Salesman?* Larry wondered. *Or musician, maybe.* But something in the stranger's stance and voice suggested officialdom. Larry couldn't quite put his finger on what it was. *Damn,* the thought crossed Larry's mind, *probably a new fire marshal.* The last fire marshal had suggested that the thousands of old business cards, photographs, and lipstick impressions on napkins and scraps of paper that covered the walls and ceiling of the old bar might be a fire hazard. Larry had argued that the paper mementos—particularly the lipstick traces—were the signature decor of the place. Women from the world over had pressed their freshly glossed lips to napkins, note-paper, and the backs of photos and business cards, and then stapled or straight-pinned them to any available bare spot of wall and even across the ceiling. It was a tradition. Traditions, Larry argued, weren't really subject to regulation. Or shouldn't be. Larry had invited the fire marshal to come by one night—any night—and see the place—and the tradition—in action, have a few drinks, enjoy the music, bring a friend if he liked— on the house, of course—before he made up his mind about the hazardous nature of the liberally kissed room. So far, the fire marshal hadn't shown back up—officially, or as Larry's "guest." Larry had wondered if he had been expected to come up with a more readily negotiable counter-offer to the fire marshal's "suggestion." The figure in the doorway wasn't the same guy, but there was nothing in the voice and the dark outline that suggested a beer-for-breakfast guy, either.

"Larry," he corrected the silhouetted figure.

"Leonardo L. Lupo?" the man articulated very precisely—again there was an air of officialdom about the way he measured out the syllables.

"Yeah," Larry squinted to try to get a better look. "What can I do for you?"

The stranger took a couple of steps inside. He was younger than his outline had made him appear. "I'm Casey Frye."

"Yeah?" Larry raised his eyebrows. "What can I do for you?" he repeated.

The young man approached the counter, stopped, and looked at Larry as if sizing him up. There was something vaguely familiar about the young man to Larry. Again, nothing he could put into words. He was sure they hadn't met before, yet the young man reminded him of someone. The silence edged just over the line into the uncomfortable zone.

"I'm not open yet," Larry said, as much to break the silence as to impart any real information.

Chapter 43

She left the message on the answering machine at his office. It wasn't a conversation that she wanted to have at all, but it certainly was not one she wanted him to have to go through at home with his new wife.

"Fred? It's Katie. Please call me when you've finished up with your last patient today. I need to talk to you about something. Casey's fine, but it does have to do with Casey. Okay. And please don't call 'til then. I'll be out."

The last part was a lie. She would not be out. But she knew him. If she hadn't said that, he would call as soon as he got the message. He might, anyway. She just wouldn't answer the phone until she knew it was the end of his day. Meanwhile, she just rehearsed it and rehearsed it over and over in her head.

"I know you won't believe this at first—you won't *want* to believe it—but it *is* true, and you need to know. I know you'll hate me for it and hate me for saying it, but I just don't know what else to do at this point. You are not Casey's biological father." Pause. Wait for explosion. Wait for disbelief. Wait for silence. Wait.

Chapter 44

Mimi Meeks held the raffle tickets in her left hand and brushed them back and forth across the underside of her perfect left breast. Her right hand twisted a strand of her hair. She stared at Blackie with the wide-eyed anticipation of a child watching someone scoop ice cream into a waffle cone. Blackie's left hand, clutching a combination wrench, flipped back and forth. With his right hand, he touched his right ear, then his chin; he reached back and touched his wallet in his back pocket. His brow furrowed, and something like alarm flitted across his face, as if he had just remembered an awful secret. He withdrew his hand, touched his right ear again, then the tip of his nose, then went for the wallet once more. His eyes widened with an unexplained delight.

The Grand Strand SOSO Club expected each of its members to sell at least fifty raffle tickets, but the Sisters of the Sea Oats had seen the body language that accompanied Mimi's shy recitation of the club's prepared sales spiel; they gave her a hundred.

Third prize was the clincher for Blackie—a Craftsman 22-drawer roll-about tool chest. If the truth be known, though, thirty seconds into Mimi's presentation, Blackie, like most men, would have bought a ticket or two if they'd been raffling off dryer lint. Second prize was a Remington 870 shotgun, and first prize was a three-day getaway trip to New York City, courtesy of Sand and Shell Travel Agency—run by two of the SOSO Club's founding members, sisters Sandy and Shelly Rivers.

Two weeks later, when Blackie's ticket was drawn as the first prize winner, he would have gladly traded his first prize for third, if he had thought about it, and if had known who had won third prize, and if Mimi hadn't been so excited for him.

"Oh, I've *always* wanted to go to New York City," she'd said to him, almost breathless with excitement, her eyes wide and staring as if she were taking in the lights of Times Square for the first time just over his shoulder. She drew her shoulders in, which in turn squeezed her breasts together, and she shivered slightly as the thrill ran through her. "Please take lots of pictures, okay? Lots. Lots and lots. And will you bring me back a souvenir?" If the souvenir she'd wanted had been the Brooklyn Bridge, traffic would still be backed up on either side of the East River. But what she wanted was a snow-globe with the Empire State Building inside it. And so it was—with all the determination of Arthur in quest of the Holy Grail—that Blackie Black boarded a jet to the Big Apple in search of a snow-globe that would make Mimi Meeks laugh and hold it in front of her and shake it and make the snow swirl and make all of Blackie's favorite sight-seeing spots shimmy and jiggle in ways that sometimes kept him awake at night.

Otherwise, New York City is not a place that

Blackie would have ever ventured to. "Sin and danger. Danger and sin. That's all it ever was, and all it'll ever be." That's what his grandfather had told him. His grandfather had passed through the great city twice—once on his way to The Great War, and once on his way back. He never furnished the details of his observations and experiences that apparently added up to sin and danger, danger and sin, but he was firm and consistent in his appraisal. He thought about his grandfather's warning as the uniformed man at the passenger screening table plucked the pocket knife from the plastic bowl into which Blackie had emptied the contents of his pockets. It had been his grandfather's Barlow knife, then his father's, and now his. It was the most tangible material link to who he used to be— "Zildjian" engraved into the backstrap of the handle—the etched letters blackened with the oils and dirt and minute pocket debris of three generations.

The man in the uniform looked at the knife, hefted it in the cradle of his fingers, and said, "I'm afraid you're not gonna be able to carry this with you on the plane."

"It's just a little whittlin' knife," Blackie said. "It was my grandfather's."

The man looked at Blackie, sized him up, and apparently settled on the word *harmless* to describe what he saw. "Put it in your bag there," he said, pointing to Blackie's worn carry-on duffle. "Way down in the bottom. How you get it back's up

172

to you. Mail it back to yourself, I'd recommend. Wherever you're goin', they might not let you keep it when to try to go through there on your way back. You need to know that."

"I 'preciate it," Blackie said. He unzipped his bag, and watched the man drop it inside. He zipped the bag closed, scooped the remaining contents of the plastic bowl up, and sorted the items—the loose change, the comb, the keys, the disposable lighter, and the wallet—back into their proper pockets. He still had forty-five minutes before boarding. "Is there a smokin' area?" he asked the man in the uniform.

"That way, and take a right," the man answered, "You'll see it."

"Thanks," Blackie answered. He tapped the pack of Winstons in his shirt pocket and headed down the hallway of the airport terminal toward the room where he would smoke his last cigarette in Myrtle Beach.

It was a fairly well-traveled knife, as knives go. When it left the Barlow Knife Company where it was born, it went by freight train to Charleston, South Carolina and then was transferred to a truck for the trip inland. After a series of shorter jaunts, including one in a wagon drawn by a mule, coincidentally *named* Barlow—though the two of them were never formally introduced—it wound up in a glass-topped display case at C.A. Guerry & Sons General Store in rural Williamsburg County, South Carolina. It was in that display case that young Jeremiah Zildjian first saw the Barlow and began to covet it. But 35¢ was a daunting sum for a fifteen-year-old boy in rural South Carolina to scrape together, and Cutter Guerry's prices were as non-negotiable as the heat that summer of 1915.

Jeremiah's parents had counted on a larger brood of children to help them work the small farm that was their home. Scarlet fever, though, had taken his younger brother and his older sister. In a corner of the property on a small rise some distance behind the house, the Zildjians marked off an area as their very own family cemetery. Two simple tombstones marked the graves of Jeremiah's brother and sister, with space between them for a third grave. Jeremiah knew the space in the middle was his. To him, the two tombstones that were already in place always looked like Death's bookends.

In 1913, the Zildjians had taken on a hired man, Wash Vickery—a name steeped in irony since he never did. Wash, that it. He did perform just enough work, however, to make his noisome attachment to their lives marginally worth having him around, and the next year they even allowed him to build a small shack in the patch of woods on the far side of the tobacco field. In those woods, Wash Vickery assembled a small still, which began to consume more and more of his time and attention until Jeremiah started to overhear his parents discussing just how ugly the encounter might become when they told ol' Wash he was going to have to leave, and exactly how they were going to get along without even the little bit of help he was still contributing to the farm's workload. Jeremiah's father was spared the confrontation when he went to Wash's shack one morning early in the summer of 1915 to find out why Wash had not turned out to help with the chores. During the night, Wash had shuffled off this mortal coil, leaving the Zildjians to dispose of his reasty remains. Briefly, Jeremiah thought that Wash might take the spot between the two tombstones, seemingly completing the set and throwing the Grim Reaper off his trail, but his parents planted the old farm hand in a far corner of the cemetery, downwind from the eternal slumber of the family's dearly departed. A couple of weeks passed before Jeremiah's father told him to go clean out the old shack and see if it might be made suitable as a storage shed. When he asked his father what he should do with Wash's stuff, his father told him to do whatever he wanted to do with it. Most of the contents were barely suitable for burning. Then Jeremiah found the jars of Wash Vickery's moonshine. Everybody knew that Cutter Guerry sold a few jars of white liquor out the back door of the store, when he could get it. Jeremiah thought about the Barlow and began to load the jars into an old wooden crate.

In Jeremiah Zildjian's hands, the Barlow gutted and skinned more catfish, rabbits, and squirrels than it could remember. It traveled with Jeremiah off to the Great War, passing twice through New York—going and coming. Though it went to war, it was never raised as a weapon against another man. In fact, the only human blood it had tasted was after Jeremiah passed it along to his son, Woodrow Wilson Zildjian, who learned the dangers of whittling with a dull knife and bore a small scar on his right kneecap all his life to remind him. With young Woodrow, the Barlow left to go to war a second time, but got no farther than New Smyrna, Florida. And now it burrowed down through the socks and underwear and extra packs of Winstons in the old duffle bag as Blackie Black— formerly Clifford Woodrow Zildjian—stubbed out his cigarette in the smoking lounge of the Myrtle Beach Airport and prepared to board his flight to New York—a place neither of them ever thought they'd end up.

Chapter 45

"I'm not here to drink," Casey said to the man behind the bar. Larry, he had said his name was. *Hinky* was the word that some of the older guys that he worked with used—vaguely suspicious; nothing you could really put your finger on or articulate, but...just not quite right somehow. There was something hinky about Larry. "Mind if I sit down a minute, though?"

"Well...like I said, I'm not open yet," Larry squinted and said.

Casey sat down on a barstool anyway.

"I'm looking for someone," he said. "Kind of a missing persons case."

"You a cop?" Larry asked and scooped up a highball glass full of ice. Picking up the beverage gun, he squirted Coke into the glass of ice and took a sip. His mouth was suddenly dry.

"Yes. Yes, I am," Casey studied the man's face. It was nothing like the face he expected to find. He tried to find something, *anything* in that face that his mother might once have found so intriguing as to risk her marriage over, but he just wasn't seeing it.

Something in the way the young man was looking at him, scanning his face like he was trying to spot something hidden beneath some sort of disguise, threw Larry off. Normally he would have been quick to ask for some identification—a badge, something—but the man's whole way of looking at him had upset the rhythm of his thinking. He struggled to regain his balance, conversationally.

"Lots of folks in and out of here. Hard to tell which ones are missing persons and which ones just *wish* they were," he tagged a half-hearted laugh on the end of it, groping for the terra firma of pleasant conversation.

Casey recognized the maneuver—distract and avoid 'til a better plan presents itself. Stall. Tap dance. He didn't have time to catch this guy's whole act.

"The thing is...the missing person *I'm* looking for...is named...Leonardo L. Lupo." He watched Larry's eyes cutting, darting, searching for a reply. "Interesting, huh?"

"Yeah," Larry said, "that's some coincidence." He took a swig of Coke.

"It gets better," Casey leaned a little forward. "He owned a bar in Key West...called Lupo's."

"Listen—" Larry began "—I don't know what you're up to or who you think you're trying to rattle—"

"Rattle?" Casey interrupted. "Are you...rattled...Larry?"

"No. I'm just sayin'—"

"Because I'll tell you the truth, Larry. I am. Rattled, I mean. A little. Not in a bad way, really. More like anxious, ya know? Like when you're *real* close to something; right on the verge, as they say. Because this is *real* important. And I'd just like it to go...you know, smooth."

"What'd this guy do?" Larry took another drink and wiped his hands on a bar towel.

"Do? It's not what he *did*, really. It's more like what might happen if I don't find him. It's not like he's in trouble or anything. But to not find him would be a very bad thing. You understand, Larry?"

"I wish I could help you, but I...I don't know what to tell you."

"Oh, you *have* helped me, Larry. Already. You're standing here in his bar, and you have his name. That's a real nice start. Now I just need you to help me clear up a few things."

Larry cleared his throat and took another sip of Coke. He tried to think of something to say— something sharp, savvy—something that would make this young man stop and reassess his air of self-confidence, but his mind was filled with a confusing blur of images like a video montage on rapid rewind.

"There's nothing wrong with changing your name," Casey's voice yanked Larry back into the moment. "Legally, that is," he continued. "In fact, it's pretty darn simple. Cost you about sixty-five, maybe seventy bucks in Florida. You can change it to whatever you like. Hell—you can be Quick-Draw McGraw, if you wanna be." A short pause. "Did you like Quick-Draw? Ba-Ba Louie? I always did. When I was a kid, I mean."

"What?" Larry was confused. He wasn't sure what cartoon characters had to do with any of

179

this.

"Doesn't matter. Anyway, the point is...anybody can change his name legally. It's only a problem when it's *not* done legally. Or when it's done to defraud. For instance, did you know that if someone, for example, assumed the identity of somebody who was a veteran, let's say..."

Jesus, Larry thought, *Lennie Lupo* was *a veteran*. Marine Corps. That's one of the things he liked about being Leonardo L. Lupo.

"...and that somebody applied for and received a loan of some sort, and veteran's preference got factored in, then that somebody might have committed…fraud?"

Larry's mind zipped back through any loans he had applied for. Veteran's preference? He didn't recall reading or hearing anything like that. But he wasn't sure.

Casey could almost see the wheels spinning in Larry's head. He pressed ahead.

"'The big one, though, is the IRS. Tax fraud. Talk about having the feds up your ass. Whew! 'Course I always say, 'What the feds don't know, won't hurt them.' How 'bout you? You see any need to bring the feds into something like that? You got a head?"

"What?" Larry was feeling more and more like he was a step behind on everything.

"Head? Bathroom? A pisser?"

"Oh. Yeah. Right back there," Larry pointed. He could use the break to sort this out, he thought.

"Great. While I'm gone, I'd appreciate it if you'd see if you can think of a *simple* way to help me find out what happened to that Leonardo L. Lupo who had a bar called Lupo's in Key West. The guy I'm looking for, ya know?" He started toward the rest room, stopped, turned back and cut his eyes around the room. "Jeez, I hope there's no feds lurkin' around, listening in. Wouldn't *that* be a bitch. Be right back."

Fuck! thought Larry. For just a moment, he thought about running out to his car, jumping in, and just driving away. *But to what,* he thought, *to where? Wait! I could still change my name. Legally. Yeah!* He heard the toilet flush. *But not before that sonuvabitch gets back here.*

Casey exited from the men's room. Paused. Looked at Larry. And smiled. Larry sighed deeply, splashed some Jack Daniels into his glass, and gave it another shot of Coke from the beverage gun.

Chapter 46

The truth of the matter is that in the South, in particular, the terms *up*town and *down*town are used pretty much interchangeably to mean "*to* town"—as in, "I'm goin' uptown to the movies," or "I'm goin' downtown to see the Christmas lights." Perhaps that's what confused Blackie Black about the New York transit system and led to his subway ride to Brooklyn. Perhaps it was the logical and systematic layout of numbered streets and avenues that makes perfect sense to the Brooklynite headed up to Manhattan or to the Manhattanite headed down through Brooklyn, but which presents itself like a grossly unremarkable maze to the mind whose sense of direction is based on streets named after Confederate generals and the daughters of the owner of the textile mill that employed your parents. At any rate, one of Blackie Black's final discoveries in life was that 25th Street in Manhattan and 25th Street in Brooklyn are two different places.

Plan B was much simpler. Rather than trying to construct a wall of dog shit at Shane Callahan's front door, Jock would go with a variation of an old Halloween prank he had read about somewhere in which country kids would put cow shit in a paper bag, place the bag on a neighbor's front porch, light the bag, knock and run. The idea, of course, was for the neighbor to see the burning bag, panic, and stomp on the bag to put out the fire, thus splattering the cow shit. *Bumpkins*, he thought. But he would use it.

In Jock's variation, he would fill a pizza box with dog shit. A pizza box was the perfect construction for him to stand it on its end in the space between the storm door and the front door. The fire was more than just a nice touch; it was a must. Fire always makes a dramatic statement. Jock figured a liberal squirt of lighter fluid along the top edge of the box would be just perfect. He had failed, however, to factor in two things: a shaky Southern boy lost in Brooklyn; and the aggressive nature of Duchess' protective instincts.

Jock had counted on Duchess' barking to draw Shane Callahan to the door, but in his plan, the barking came as a response to Jock's ringing the doorbell, right after he lit the pizza box.

The Retributor was all about restoring *order*. It was imperative that every action went according to plan. Outside the carefully crafted comic book world, however, things can go wrong so quickly.

Damn dog, he silently cursed. *Stupid, fucking dog.*

It startled him. Duchess must have been just on the other side of the door. As soon as he had opened the storm door, the first sharp bark jolted him, and he flinched as if he had been bitten. Suddenly, everything shifted into fast forward. He set the box filled with dog shit on its edge, pulled out the can of lighter fluid, and clawed at the recessed plastic nozzle with his thumb nail. *Bark!*

"'Scuse me?"

The voice behind him startled him again. And made no sense. *Bark!* A scene from a movie flashed through his head. *Deliverance*? No. That Tennessee Williams movie? What was the name of it? *Bark! Bark!*

"'Scuse me!"

There it was again. He turned, the lighter fluid can in his hand. *Bark!* There at the base of the steps was a man—all twitches and drawl and wide eyes. *Bark! Bark!*

Who the hell? This was all wrong, suddenly surreal.

The man twitched again and began frantically touching his face and ears as if to make sure that *he* was really standing there on a sidewalk, asking directions from a man with a black hood over his head, and not trapped in some bizarre dreamscape himself. "Can you tell me if the Arlin'ton Hotel is somewhere 'round here?"

Hotel? he thought. The yokel punched the first part of HO-tel like it should have been followed by "down." *Where the hell did he come from? What's he doing here?* He turned back and squeezed the can of lighter fluid, watched the stream arc and splatter along the top edge of the box—some of it soaking in, some of it running down the side. *Bark! Bark!*

The barking grew louder, more insistent, and claws scratched and slapped at the inside base of the door. A voice inside yelled, "Duchess!" Footsteps.

184

Jock pulled out the lighter and flicked it to life.

Bark! Bark! Bark! The clawing at the door became frantic.

"I seem to've got myself turned around somehow, an'—" the bumpkin was still just standing there. It made no sense.

As he touched the flame to the box, everything seemed to happen at once.

The box top ignited with a soft *whoosh*, and flames shot up along the front door. The door flew open, and instantly, Duchess was leaping through the flames at his face. He was backing up, still in mid-crouch, and felt himself falling backwards, while at the same time reaching out to grab the beast lunging at him. He managed to deflect the animal in mid-leap, sending it crashing into the chest of the wide-eyed stranger at the foot of the steps. The hood twisted sideways, and he couldn't see.

Shane Callahan shouted and kicked the blazing box outside, right on top of him. He sprawled onto his back amongst a shower of sparks and burning cardboard and dog shit, reached up and yanked the hood from his head. It was then, as he saw the dog—teeth bared, strings of slobber flying from its mouth—bounding back up the steps toward him, that he pulled the Savage .32 and swung it toward the dog.

The first round caught Duchess in the right jowl, right at the top of the steps. She yelped, leapt sideways, and scrambled for footing to get back to

185

her attacker.

It wasn't until later, when he counted the bullets left in the clip, that he realized he had fired three times.

In the great, unspoken Fight or Flight Cosmic Betting Pool, hardly anyone would have plunked down a sawbuck on Blackie Black to Fight. Blackie himself, given the chance to get in on the action before that night, would likely have twitched and jerked and then laid his money down on Flight. But you never know until it happens.

At first, Blackie wasn't sure who or what was out to get him, man or beast. *Sin and danger. Danger and sin.* His grandfather's words flashed in his head. Amid the fire and the shouts and the dog shit and the snarls, the wild eyes and the snapping jaws and the blood and the gunshots, Jeremiah Zildjian's old Barlow knife flashed open and trembled in the grip of Blackie's good right wrench-turning hand.

The second shot tore through Duchess' neck, and she crumpled. But bullet number two was not done yet. After it passed through the soft tissue of the dog's throat, it thudded squarely into Blackie's sternum. It took his breath away and took him to his knees, just as the man with the gun scrambled down the steps toward him. *Sin and danger, danger and sin* coming to finish him off. Blackie came around with the knife in kind of a roundhouse blow, and he felt the blade lodge solidly into something. He would never know what.

Jock howled and shoved the barrel of the .32 against the forehead of the strange crazy man from the movie whose title he couldn't remember, and—*bang!*—the man jerked backwards away from him. Jock lurched down the last steps and tried to outrun the blinding pain in his left thigh.

Blackie lay on the sidewalk, a star-shaped, blackened hole in his forehead. He twitched. He heard a voice—it seemed a long way off and hollow-sounding, as if someone was hollering down a tunnel—"Duchess!" and then he twitched no more. Later, Mimi Meeks would say to somebody, "I hope he got to keep the dog when they both got to heaven."

Chapter 47

Casey Frye stood and looked at himself in the mirror, trying to picture himself thirty years older. He squinted to create little crinkle lines around his eyes. He wondered about his hairline. *Donald Ray Black*, he thought. Larry Lupo had finally told him the whole story. The bad news was that he was back to Square One. Well, maybe not all the way back to Square One. Close, though. Square Two, maybe. The good news was that in thirty years he wouldn't be looking in the mirror and seeing Donald Ray Black.

A con man, he thought. *My old man's some kinda fuckin' con man.*

He tried to figure out what the exact angle was—the scam. Lenny Lupo essentially had traded lives with this guy. Why? Where was the payoff? Sure, he had gotten the used car lot—Li'l Cricket Discount Motors—which was really all Don Black had left, but in exchange, he had handed over the bar. Casey couldn't see any real profit. *Maybe he's just a really incompetent con man*, he thought.

He thought about calling Debbie. He ought to, he knew. At the beginning, he had considered fabricating some story about who he was looking for and why, but he knew that sooner or later she would have to know the truth. Better sooner. The odd thing was that he wasn't embarrassed for himself; he worried about what Debbie—or more truthfully, Debbie's parents—would think about his mother. His mother had kissed him on the cheek and told him that was gallant of him, but not to worry about her or what anyone thought of her. Gallant.

"I don't think anybody really uses that word any more, Mom," he'd told her.

"Maybe it's just that hardly anybody *is* gallant anymore," she'd replied.

I'll call her in a little while, he thought, *and maybe the Chief, too*. After he'd figured out a plan. After he'd figured out where the hell Haversham, Georgia was and what he was going to do when he got there.

Chapter 48

Okay. He had been to the Village, had a little bit too much to drink, and decided to walk it off. He was down around Tribeca when he stepped into an alley to take a piss. That's when the guy shoved him against the wall. He'd had a knife; he was Latino. Demanded his money, but then the guy had grabbed his crotch. That's when he started to fight back. And that's when the guy had stabbed him. Yeah. That was his story. That's what he would tell them to explain the wound.

Jock shifted on the gurney where he lay in the treatment room, and the paper sheet beneath him crinkled. The cops would want a description; the nurse had already said they'd have to notify the police. Mentally, he recreated the face of the Latino kid in the silver boom-thunka-boom BMW. He would do nicely. The wound in his left thigh throbbed, but it was a dull pain now, not the piercing, lightning stabs like earlier. The pain medication they'd given him was kicking in. He couldn't allow it to take over, though. He had to keep his wits about him. Figure out what had gone wrong. Puzzle it out; that would keep the mind working.

It had started out fine. People at the dog park had actually been pleasant to him, appreciative of the guy in the dark blue coveralls with DSNY stenciled on the back, who could walk around and smile even as he scooped up their pooches' droppings.

"Good boy!" he'd said to that big Airedale after he'd made a particularly impressive deposit. "Good boy!" he'd smiled and scooped it up, deposited it in the five-gallon bucket. The Airedale cocked its bearded chin and wagged its stubby tail. The lady holding the big dog's leash had smiled at him as if to say, "Amazing. Picking up dog shit and still smiling." He'd smiled back and moved on.

With the bucket over half full, he had left the dog run area and moved to a wooded area of Prospect Park. He had peeled the dark blue, iron-on rectangle of fabric with the DSNY on it from the back of the coveralls, but he'd kept the coveralls on. No need to take chances when you're messing around with dog shit. Same with the rubber gloves. Better safe than shitty.

He'd troweled the foul mix into the large pizza box 'til it was almost full and then closed the lid. *Fresh and still warm in thirty minutes or your next box of shit is free*, he'd thought and laughed at his own joke.

He'd checked his inventory. The black mask/bag, of course. The small NYC "Curb Your Dog" sign that he had taken off a fence along the side of a church, and directly beneath which some unknown asshole in need of a serious attitude adjustment had allowed his dog to take a dump. On the back side of the sign he had already lettered the message: *We're not taking any more of your shit.* He signed it with the symbolic lightning bolt *R*. The

191

can of Zippo lighter fluid. The lighter. A thin-bladed putty knife, in case he had to slip the catch on the storm door. And the Savage .32, tucked into the waistband of his black trousers beneath the coveralls.

It was dark as he had approached Shane Callahan's brownstone. No one else on the street at the moment. He had stepped into a driveway, shifted the .32 from his inside waistband to the pocket of the coveralls. He removed the lighter fluid and lighter from the black bag and put them into the breast pocket. He laid the sign flat on top of the pizza box, stuck the putty knife into his right hip pocket, and flipped the black bag inside out. One last look, up and down the street. The coast was clear. He slipped the bag over his head and aligned the eye holes. He picked up the box, moved swiftly down the sidewalk and up the steps of the house.

Jock had set the sign down in the corner of the small porch and propped it up. He tried the storm door and was pleased to find it unlocked. As he pulled it open a little more, it squeaked. That's when Duchess barked. And everything had started to go terribly wrong. And that strange, wide-eyed bumpkin—

"Excuse me."

Jock jumped. He had closed his eyes. *When did I close my eyes*, he wondered. An officer stood beside the gurney. He looked overweight and over-tired.

"You the guy that got stabbed?"

"Yeah," Jock answered. "You catch the guy already?"

"What kinda drugs they givin' *you*?" the cop responded with a half-smirk, half-grin. "You up for a few questions?"

"Yeah. I think I can manage that." He followed the cop's eyes to the black bag sitting on the one chair in the curtained treatment area. He knew the cop was going to pick up the bag so that he could sit in the chair, and for an instant, he felt his chest tighten up. Suddenly, the curtain parted and a young Indian woman stepped into the room.

"Mr. Dejohnette? I'm Doctor Singh. How are you feeling?"

"A little dopey. A little bit lucky to be here."

"Well, we're going to fix you up." She turned to the officer. "He's probably not going to be able to do much talking while we're working. Can you come back in about twenty minutes?"

"I'll go interrogate a cup of coffee. Be back shortly," and he pushed through the opening in the curtain.

"Could you do me a favor?" Jock asked the doctor.

"What's that?"

"Could you put my bag of groceries there—" he pointed to the chair, "—underneath my gurney here? I don't want them to get in the way, and I don't want to lose them."

"Sure," she said, and she swung the bag onto the shelf under the rollaway. "Looks like you *were* lucky," she said as she looked at the chart, at an X-ray, and then at the wound on his thigh. "No major damage. But we are going to have to get that piece of metal—part of a blade, it looks like—out. And that might be a little uncomfortable for you."

"I'm not going to have to be admitted, am I?" he asked. "I really need to get back home tonight. I got no one to look after my dog at home."

"We'll see," Dr. Singh said. "Depends on how this goes."

Gotta stay awake, he thought. *Gotta keep an eye on the groceries.*

Chapter 49

Sitting in the living room of Abbie Black Flagg's home was about as comfortable as sitting at a computer in the parlor of a nunnery to have cybersex.

"I believe if you have information concerning my brother's whereabouts you are required by law to furnish me that information, Mr....Fryer, is it?" Abbie looked at Casey as if she were looking at a servant. She cut an icy glance at her husband Julius, as if that were his cue to back her up on the point by quoting a specific volume, chapter, and statute. He merely shifted in his chair and cleared his throat.

"It's *Frye*, Mrs. Flagg, and—no—I don't believe there is any such legal requirement. But I can assure you that your brother is alive and well. He has changed his name, I believe."

"My father would roll over in his grave. Well, surely, you can tell me where he is. If there is no legal obligation, surely, you must recognize the moral one."

"Well, ma'am, I'm afraid all of that is entirely up to your brother. He has been very helpful, and I was just hoping that you might be able to tell me anything about the disposal of the used car lot he ran—if, after he left, anyone contacted you about any of the details; where they might have called from; anything like that?"

"It seems to me that if you are going to be

less than forthcoming with me, then I have very little reason to share any information *I* might have with you. So...if that's all, Mr. Fryer—" he was sure now that she was doing it on purpose—"I believe we have little else to talk about. My husband will see you to the door," she said as she rose from her seat. Clearly, he was dismissed.

When they got to the front door, Julius Flagg stepped outside with Casey. He pulled the door almost closed and lowered his voice to a near whisper.

"Somebody said—this has been years ago now—but somebody said he might be working in a bar."

For a moment, Casey was disappointed. He was hoping for something he *didn't* know. Almost as an afterthought he asked, "Do you know where?"

"Charlotte, I think, is what they said."

Casey felt a quick rush. It was cut short by Abbie's voice from within.

"Julius!"

"Coming, dear."

"Thanks," Casey said quietly.

Julius just smiled and stepped back inside. Just as the door was closing, Casey saw the smile disappear. Obviously, Julius Flagg was a man reduced to taking any small victory he could, whenever and wherever he could.

Charlotte, thought Casey. Square three? Now he would call Chief Singleton.

Chapter 50

Two blocks away from Shane Callahan's house, Jock had sat down behind a dumpster at the rear of a Korean grocery. He had to think through the pain and come up with some answers quickly. He touched the wound on his leg. *Not as much blood as there could be*, he thought. *That's good.* But he could feel *some*thing in there. He knew he was going to have to find an emergency room, and he knew there would be lots of questions. And, *Jesus*, he smelled like shit.

He pulled the coveralls off and tore a wide strip of cloth from one leg. He used the cloth to bind the wound as tightly as he could stand. Every time he moved, he could feel something there in his leg cutting at the tissue around it, and the pain shot down his leg and then back up. He saw an old plastic grocery bag on the ground. He stuffed the torn, bloodied coveralls into the bag, tied the top, and tossed it into the dumpster.

Remove yourself from the area, he thought. Which emergency room? NYU Downtown Hospital. *Can I make it that far?* he wondered. He would have to. How far? What—two blocks to the subway? Three? The N or the R. Then ten stops maybe? Yes, he could do that. He *would* do it. *Oh, fuck! The gun.* What to do with the gun? Figure it out on the way. Sirens and people down around Callahan's house. He could hear them.

A block from the subway, a small Mexican

market was open. He ducked inside, tried not to limp or wince from the pain. He glanced around. *Cheerios!* Cheerios would do nicely. And something for heft—decoy weight to draw attention away from the Cheerios. Dog food. He picked up two cans. He set his purchases on the counter, noticed the tubes of glue, and asked for one. He paid in cash, and asked the old woman at the register to double bag it, please.

Outside, he slipped the grocery bags inside the black tote bag and held the bag on his left side to cover any telltale signs of his wound. Fortunately, his trousers were black and the cloth binding seemed to have stemmed most of the flow of blood.

He had no sooner made it to the platform when the Uptown N train arrived, and he slipped into a car with only one old Asian couple sitting near the front. He moved to the rear of the car and sat down. As the train pulled away, he carefully opened the box of Cheerios, reached inside and took out a small handful. He popped them into his mouth and chewed as he carefully withdrew the .32 and slipped it down into the middle of the cheery little Os. He removed the cap from the tube of glue, bent the end of the nozzle back and forth until it snapped off, and squeezed a line of adhesive across the inside of the top tab. He folded the tab down and held it in place for the glue to dry. There. Safe and sound. Like a prize in a box of Cracker Jacks.

He tossed the tube of glue under the seat in front of him, and started to count down the number of stops left. He would make it. He knew he would. The train rattled and his leg throbbed. The train pulled into 4th Ave./9th St. Eight more stops to go. Or was it nine?

Chapter 51

Casey dialed Chief Clarence Singleton's home phone number. Clarence Singleton was the Chief of the ten-man Ashers Grove Police Department—now one man short due to Casey's absence.

There are pros and cons to working for a small town police department.

The pay is less—often considerably less—than that of the big police departments. Can't be helped. It's a tax base thing. Do the math. The turnover rate is high. That is tied to the pay rate and limited opportunities for advancement and specialization. Young officers often take jobs in small departments and bide their time until they can "move up," as many of them see it, to a larger department.

On the up side—in the year and a half since Casey had come on the Ashers Grove Police Department and had been taken under the AquaVelva-scented wing of Chief Singleton, he had investigated a homicide—two shots from a .22 pistol fired by one drunk into the chest of his equally drunk cousin; he had worked an emotionally-charged traffic fatality in which the wife of one of the town's two dentists had struck and killed a twelve-year old girl on a bicycle; and he had made several felony arrests, including the capture of two out-of-state fugitives in mid-burgle of a local drugstore. He had processed crime scenes, addressed an elementary school assembly, and assisted in the raid of a small-time meth lab.

In a small department, you handle it all—whether it's an unruly drunk pissing into the mouth of the cannon beside the VFW, a domestic dispute over who drank the last Old Milwaukee, or a murder. You are your own detective, your own crime scene technician, your own juvenile officer, your own community relations/crime prevention specialist, your own accident reconstructionist, your own SWAT team, if need be. You're it. You and your partner, if you're lucky.

Large departments—for all their big budgets, TV cop drama-inspiring, puff and profile—relegate their new officers, typically, to *years* of mind-numbing, report-taking, citation-issuing, first response grunt work, all to be handed over to some "specialist" just when it's starting to get interesting. A typical two year veteran of a small department has gotten to do more genuine no-shit interesting police work than a five year veteran in most big cities. He or she *had* to.

The small department may not have the budget for all the latest technological law enforcement gizmos, but it does have a computer or two, at least. Thus, it has access to NCIC, LEIN, NLETS, and other really handy information exchange networks that won't let the incurably curious civilian population play. Even among the police rank and file, access is restricted, supposedly, to those with "a need to know" and only "to perform their official duties." Like most things in life, interpretation of that restriction is somewhat subjective and elastic.

In the really giant departments, it's just impossible to monitor and scrutinize every inquiry. The medium-sized departments are probably the strictest when it comes to adherence. Lots of bureaucrats with their eyes on other bureaucrats and by-the-book asshole shift commanders who think that nit-picking is a leadership quality. Small departments tend to become like large families. If weird Uncle Delbert embarrasses the whole family by showing up on the front page of the local paper with his trousers around his ankles and a trout in each hand, you'll denounce him as the black sheep, but if you can get to him before the photographer does, you *will* tell the curious onlookers that Aunt Sally told him to change his pants and go get 'em two fish sandwiches from McDonalds, and—bless his heart—he must've gotten confused. You have to look out for one another. Chief Clarence Singleton reasoned that Casey Frye *really* had "a need to know" where his biological father was so that he could get his operation and get back to work, so that he could "perform his official duties." It was just a matter of interpretation.

Chapter 52

When the officer who had first come into Jock Dejohnette's treatment room learned that there was evidence to be collected—whatever it was that had to be removed from the wound—he called for a detective to come take over. No need to complicate the chain of custody. Plus, that meant an extra trip and additional paperwork—the kind of stuff that the gold shields got paid extra for, he figured.

Detective Antonio Bozzone was in no hurry to get home. He sat in the chair in the corner of the treatment room and thoughts of retirement rattled around in his head among the sounds and smells of the E.R.

"There it is," Dr. Singh said. "Looks like part of the blade. Snapped off. The tip's lodged in the femur pretty solidly."

"Try not to mess it up getting it out, if you can help it," the detective offered.

He handed her a 2-oz. plastic evidence collection jar with the screw-top cap loosened but still on. He had already placed a sterile gauze pad in the bottom of the jar.

"I'll try," Dr. Singh answered. "Depends on how good a grip I can get on it the first time. And how stubborn it is. It's a good thing his thighs are so skinny. Otherwise, I'd have to send him to surgery to get it out."

"Hey—I'm *in the room*, ya know," Jock piped up. He lay on his back on the treatment table, his right forearm draped across his eyes.

"Hand me those surgical pliers," Dr. Singh spoke to the nurse who was assisting her.

"Pliers?!" Jock was feeling glib, but feeling no pain. "What're you doing down there—tightening my nuts?"

Dr. Singh had dealt with the sexual jabs and double entendres of male patients, as well as male colleagues before. "If I were tightening your nuts, Mr. Dejohnette, I would have asked for a wrench. A very small one."

Detective Bozzone laughed, and Jock gritted his teeth as he felt the pressure of Dr. Singh's extraction technique.

She had turned a small stainless steel kidney tray upside down on his thigh and braced the pliers against the bottom as a fulcrum. When she gripped the piece of blade with the teeth of the pliers, she pushed down against the tray, and the embedded tip of the Barlow blade popped neatly from the bone, intact. The nurse unscrewed the top of the evidence jar, and Dr. Singh dropped the piece of blade inside. With tweezers, she picked up another square of sterile gauze and nestled it on top of the piece of metal. The nurse twisted the lid closed and handed the jar to Dr. Singh. She turned and placed it into the open palm of Detective Bozzone.

"There you are, detective," she said. "Now if you will give us a few minutes to close up and dress our patient here, the two of you can chat the rest of the night away, if you like." She smiled.

Detective Bozzone slipped the jar into the side pocket of his sport coat and stepped through the curtain.

Chapter 53

Casey met with Dr. Strejc to discuss his case. There were some more tests. He was running out of time. Dr. Strejc told him that they only had three or four weeks—six, tops—to either do this—the transplant procedure—or for Casey to go ahead with the traditional surgery. *Traditional*.

What an odd word choice, Casey thought. *Welcome! Welcome, everyone, to our traditional candle-lighting, tree-trimming, and DE-nutting festivities!* After they hung his balls on the highest bough, perhaps there would be caroling and wassail.

Since future parenthood was an issue, as a hedge against the clock running out, Dr. Strejc suggested that Casey think seriously about using the services of a sperm bank—that he make several "deposits" which could later be used for artificial insemination procedures, if need be. Assuming his sperm was still viable.

Casey didn't know which he looked forward to more: talking about it to Debbie, or the lusty episodes of clinical masturbation themselves. He pictured himself standing on the sidewalk in front of a cinderblock clinic with a huge blazing pink neon sign: *ACME XXX Sperm Bank*. Painted on the blacked-out windows were things like "Private Booths" and "Peepshows 25¢." An inflatable love doll, dressed in a nurse's uniform with white stocking and garter belt, was propped in one window. He pictured himself standing there and shouting to throngs of passers-by, "I'm going inside to masturbate now! It's okay, though. It's traditional!"

Dr. Strejc gave him yet another brochure and the names of two clinics.

Casey thought of Debbie and how awkward sex had become since his diagnosis. Their sex life had always been free and easy. Fun, even. She was on the Pill, but at one point, she had asked, "Should you wear a condom, do you think?" When he had asked why, she just shrugged and said, "I don't know. It was just a thought."

He thought he knew what she was thinking—why she wasn't relaxed like she used to be—why she practically braced herself for his ejaculation and then was so quick to excuse herself to go to the bathroom. He was shooting a contaminated load—killer semen laced with cancer cooties. It made sense.

He asked Dr. Strejc if it was possible to infect a partner somehow because of his condition. Could tiny testicular cancer saboteurs invade a defenseless vagina and morph themselves into, say, cervical cancer?

"No," Dr. Strejc assured him, "there is nothing, clinically, to suggest that such a transmission has ever occurred."

Casey was just about to ask him if he had a brochure with *that* in it when Dr. Strejc added, "Still—a condom's not a bad idea."

Chapter 54

Jock sat in a wheelchair, the bag of groceries on his lap. He wore a pair of scrub pants that they had given him after they had finished suturing and dressing his leg. They'd had to cut his pants off. He eyed the brown paper bag that the detective held now. His pants were inside the bag.

Brown paper bags work better than plastic bags for storing evidence like blood-soaked pants. Left inside a plastic bag, the blood will putrefy and begin to break down. Brown paper breathes and allows the bloodstains to dry. Once dried, the blood can be reconstituted easily for testing later.

Jock was more than a little agitated that the detective had the pants. He was trying to strike a balance between pleasant and nonchalant, but when the detective introduced himself, what came bubbling to the surface was his natural penchant for smart-ass.

"As in Tony, Tony, *Buzz-on-ee*; banana, fana, *fuzz-on-ee*?"

"Gee—I never heard *that* before," Detective Bozzone responded dryly. "I hope that knife wound doesn't put a damper on your *stand-up* act." He flipped open a notebook and plucked his pen from his shirt pocket.

"Is this going to take long?" Jock sighed. "It's already been a *really* long night."

"I'll make it as quick as possible, but the fresher the whole thing is in your head, the better.

Why don't you start earlier in the evening and then lead up to the assault."

Jock recounted the story he had rehearsed. He had gone to the Village, had too much to drink, and decided to walk it off. He had stepped into an alley to take a piss, and that's when this guy—this Hispanic guy—had tried to rob him. There was a struggle; he was stabbed; he stumbled to the hospital. That was it. He started to provide a more detailed description of his attacker, but the detective interrupted him.

"Where were you drinking?"

"Where?"

"Yeah. In the Village. Which bar?"

"There were a few of them, actually. I didn't stay any one place too long."

"I understand. Which ones, though? Just so I can start to put all this together. You never know—this guy may have followed you out of one of the bars. Maybe somebody'll recognize the description."

"I don't think anybody followed me."

There was a long pause. The detective held his pen poised above his notebook. He raised his eyebrows, waiting. Jock thought quickly.

"Elbow Room," Jock offered.

"Yeah? Anybody good playing last night?"

"I, uh, I wasn't paying all that much attention. I was drinking."

"Ah. Did you set out to get drunk? Was that the idea?"

"Not really."

"Okay. Where else?"

"Um, Chumley's."

"On Bedford."

"Yeah."

"Busy?"

"Yeah. Pretty crowded."

"Anywhere else? You said 'a few' places."

"Some pub. I don't remember the name."

"Feelin' pretty good by that point, huh?"

"Yeah, I guess I was."

"So, which way'd you walk?"

"Oh. Just came down Greenwich. Cut over toward City Hall."

"Where was that?"

"Murray, I think."

"And this happened where, again?"

"Just down from there, I think. A block, maybe."

"So between Greenwich and West Broadway."

"I think. Maybe the next block."

"Okay. So down Greenwich to Murray..."

"Yeah. I think it was Murray."

"Then east. Between Greenwich and West Broadway or *maybe* Church?"

"I wasn't paying a lot of attention."

"And then after it happened, you, what—ran here?"

"Yeah. Best I could."

"All the way past West Broadway or

Church, Broadway, across City Hall Park?"

"Three, four blocks. Something like that."

"Why didn't you call 911?"

"I just started running. I just wanted to get out of there, ya know?"

"What about your groceries?"

"What?"

"Well, I'm guessing you didn't stop and shop on your way to the hospital, right?"

"No. Of course not."

"You didn't mention stopping along the way. On Greenwich."

"No. No, I got 'em earlier."

"And lugged them around with you all night while you were drinking?"

"I just...got 'em earlier. I didn't want to forget the dog food."

"Ah. So what kinda dog you got? I had a cat. Inherited it, actually, from my ex-wife. Still—you get attached, ya know? Just had to have it put to sleep a few weeks ago. Sad thing."

"Yeah. That's rough."

"So what kind?"

"Jack Russell."

"Boy, those things are hyper, aren't they? About half-crazy, I understand. All the in-breeding or something."

"He's...he's not a bad dog."

"I, personally, don't think people ought to have dogs in the city. Not good for the dogs. Not good for the sidewalks. Ya know?"

"Yeah."

"Probably thought you were a tourist."

"I beg your pardon?"

"The perp. Guy who mugged you. Usually only tourists carry those bags around." He pointed at the black "I ♥ New York" bag on Jock's lap. "Looks like that one's seen better days."

"What?"

"Looks like you got a couple of rips in it. On the side. Noticed 'em earlier."

"Oh. Yeah. It's been around."

"Okay. I'll do some checking around. I may have to give you a call—come by, maybe—in a day or two. Just to clear up anything that comes up. 'Course if we get our hands on anybody, I'll let you know. By the way—you got a work number, in case I need to get up with you there?"

"No. Not really."

"Unemployed? What do you do?"

"I'm a cartoonist."

"Oh, yeah? Animated stuff like Saturday mornings or comic books?"

"Magazines."

"When I was a kid, I used to love The Flash. And Sergeant Rock. Kid Colt. Now they got, what—Ren and Stimpy, shit like that? So…you work for one of those outfits like that?"

"No. More like freelance."

"Yeah? And you can make a living doing that?"

"I do temp work, too."

212

"Ah. Yeah—that makes sense."

"Can I go home now? Get some sleep?"

"Sure. No problem. I just need your shirt before you go."

"My shirt?"

"Yeah. Here—I got a top to match your pants there for you."

"Why do you need my shirt?"

"You never know. Guy might've left a strand of hair or two on there. Some blood. You said you struggled, right? You never know. All this DNA stuff they're doin' now—it's magic. You want me to hold your bag for you while you—"

"No," Jock cut him off. He hesitated just a moment, then pulled the shirt off.

Detective Bozzone handed him the scrub top, took the black shirt, and dropped it in the bag with the cut-up pants.

"I'll be in touch," Detective Bozzone said, as he folded his notebook and replaced his pen in his pocket. "Maybe you can draw us a picture of the guy." He slipped the notebook into his inside coat pocket. *Something's not right*, he thought, as he turned and headed for the door. *Don't know what yet. But something.*

Fuckin' dog, Jock thought. He slipped the scrub top on. *Fuckin' dogs and fuckin' hayseeds.* He wheeled himself toward the door and wondered why he had to get the one cop in the city who seemed to actually give a shit about a simple mugging.

Chapter 55

Casey had told his mom that he would come by and fill her in on what he'd found out. As he drove there, he wondered if anybody ever knew anybody else. Really knew them. What they were when they prowled naked and alone through the darkest and seediest side streets of their own private Tijuanas. What they were capable of when tossed into the middle of the gladiatorial arena to face the Seven Deadly Sins, with nothing but their genitals and a smile. What, if anything, they would trade their mothers' last smile for.

Though Casey didn't know it at the time, and though it wasn't couched in precisely those terms, that was basically Fred Frye's end of the conversation, as well, when Katie told him about the secret she had hid from him since the day she had told him she was pregnant. His words stung her—not because they inflicted any new wounds, but because they salted the wounds she had already inflicted on herself. You can only beat yourself up for so long. Then you either pass out, wear out, or go numb. It's mostly up to others to finish you off. Or leave you to deal with the pain yourself.

She was dealing with it through vodka martini therapy, occasional unscheduled crying jags, and the kind of blockbuster denial that must have given rise to that ubiquitous, big yellow smiley face.

Casey thought about Larry Lupo down in Key West and the way, even after he'd confessed it all—right down to his true birth date and social security number—he had said, "But you need to know and understand this: Even if you find him— no matter what *he* wants—I'm not going back. I'm Larry Lupo. I like being this Larry Lupo that I am. This place didn't come without problems. But I worked it out. All of it. For the first time in my life, I made it work. Just me. You might think it's all a sham. It might not look like much to you, but believe me—it's everything. And I'm not going back."

Had he been in the guru business, Casey might have told him: Life can be many things, but never false. Life is living, *being*, and by its very nature, that which *is* is true. The thing that is doing the living may shroud itself in falsehood or may practice falsehood, but that which it is doing is real and therefore true. One may adopt a pseudonym and think or even convince oneself that he is living a false life, but the life he lives is inescapably real. It is not a false life—a *pseudovita*—it is absolutely real life, just under false pretenses. A butterfly is still leading a catepiller's life; he is just sporting snazzier duds and riding the wind currents that he used to dream of when he spent all morning tying his shoes and watching out for early birds. Any spider will tell you, though: a butterfly tastes just like catepiller.

Instead, Casey just told the new and improved Larry Lupo that he wasn't out to take anything away from him. But, he did tell him, he

215

might want to talk to a good lawyer about a very discreet—out-of-state, maybe?—legal name change. If you're going to *be* Larry Lupo, he told him, why not go the whole nine yards?

Casey pulled into his mother's driveway, got out, and walked around back to the small, fenced-in plot of garden and lawn. Through the ivy-covered, wrought iron gate he saw Katie standing with a garden hose in one hand, a martini glass in the other, and an almost painfully wide smile on her face.

"Hi, Mom!" he said.

And she started to cry.

Chapter 56

Detectives Dorothy Thorn and Randall Ring from the 78th Precinct, Brooklyn South, arrived at the crime scene formerly known as Shane Callahan's house.

Dorothy Thorn was an African-American woman—fourteen years on the police department—with a penchant for planting her hands on her hips, and wrinkling and turning her nose up like she had suddenly gotten a whiff of a disgusting aroma at people and situations she didn't care for. Randall Ring was a tall, prematurely white-haired man of Austrian descent—sixteen years on the force. He had a huge, bushy white moustache. Around people and situations that he found unpleasant, he had a tendency to stand ramrod stiff—knees locked, his right foot at a perfect right angle to the center of his left foot, head tilted slightly back—and look down his nose as he twisted the left end of his moustache between his left thumb and forefinger. The two of them spent a lot of time in those poses when they were together. Still—as a team, they put together some nice investigative casework.

As they approached the taped-off scene, Dorothy spoke to a uniform officer who was helping to secure the scene.

"Whadda we got here?" she asked.

The officer stretched his neck to the right, trying to pop a crick, and answered, "One body, white male—nobody seems to know who he is, where he comes from. One body, brown dog—belongs to the house here. Both of 'em look like multiple GSWs. One witness, victim, something—owner of the house and the dog. Looks like he mighta shit all over the entire scene. Have fun."

Detective Thorn wrinkled her nose. Detective Ring had sauntered up to the edge of the taped perimeter. He struck his pose and surveyed the mess on the other side of the tape.

Chapter 57

Until he had discovered the disturbing lump on his right testicle, Casey Frye had never taken a sick day at work since he had come to Ashers Grove. Still, he only went into this with twenty-six vacation/holiday/sick days on the books. With twenty-one work days in a monthly work cycle, that meant just over a month for surgery, recovery, everything. Not to mention the time he was taking to look for Lennie Lupo.

It was already remarkable to him that, considering his situation, he hadn't gotten just a bunch of sympathetic looks and his walking papers. Most employers, he knew, would have already cut their losses. If he found that remarkable, he was amazed when, as he sat in Chief Singleton's office, the Chief told him that several of the guys—his fellow officers—had volunteered to donate their own sick days to him, if need be. Some people looked at the close-knit police subculture and saw a "Blue Wall of Silence." From inside, though, it was a Big Blue Lifeboat when you were dog-paddling for your life.

On top of that, the Chief had found Donald Rayfield Black—or at least *a* Donald Rayfield Black—same date of birth. Not in Charlotte, however, like they'd thought. In South Carolina. Myrtle Beach. He had an address and had requested a copy of the DL photo.

Clarence Singleton had, in fact, found Black

first in the North Carolina DMV files. But that license had expired. He figured that meant he had moved out of state.

With the Key West connection in mind, the Chief returned to NLETS—the National Law Enforcement Telecommunications System—on the computer and tried the state of Florida. Nothing. He decided just to walk his inquiry up the east coast...for starters. He came up empty in Georgia. But then, the Palmetto State coughed up a hit.

Casey had never been to Myrtle Beach. Like Key West, though—another tourist town. Made sense, he thought.

After her tearful recounting of the conversation with Fred, Katie Frye had insisted that Casey take her VISA card and her Exxon gas card to help out with expenses. Casey realized that he was still, at some level, disappointed...pissed off... feeling betrayed...or *some*thing by his mother's secret. He hadn't sorted it out and really dealt with it yet. He was torn about using the cards. Torn, because he wasn't sure of his motives either for accepting her help or for refusing it. If he used the cards, was he doing it to make her pay for what she had done? If he refused to use them, was he rejecting her help out of spite? It all swirled around in his head like a fog.

He did know one thing. He could use some financial help. He was driving to Myrtle Beach. And tourist towns, he had learned in Key West, can get expensive.

Chapter 58

Woody sat at the corner table in the Strike Two. He sipped his Cuba Libre, set it down, and looked at it.

"What?!" he said, in that voice that only he and his pals could hear. His pal Alky waited for his ice cubes to settle and just looked back. It was that look you get from an old friend just before he tells you he can't lend you any more money if you're just going to just keep handing it over to your bookie.

Woody reached into his shirt pocket, pulled out a pack of cigarettes, and snapped it down upright on the table beside the glass. The smokes stood there at attention, clearly feeling awkward, unwelcome. Woody reached out with his forefinger and nudged the pack backwards, flat onto its back.

"Relax," he said. "Pay no attention to Alky here. He just hates to see me have a good time if he can't claim full credit for it."

A tear of condensation slid down the glass and was quickly sucked up by the thirsty coaster.

"Yeah," Woody went on, "I invited him here. The whole pack. He was just standing around on the shelf down at the Korean market, okay? Be nice. He's good smokes."

Alky glanced over at Depression slumped in the chair to Woody's right. They exchanged a what-the-hell eyebrow shrug.

Woody flipped open the top of the pack and eased one of the tightly packed cigarettes out. The others shifted a little, grateful for the extra room. Woody hung the cigarette between his lips, leaned forward, and borrowed a bit of flame from the candle on the table. He took a drag and blew a plume of smoke up toward the dim track lighting.

"Look—" he began, "—I *know* I should be happy. I mean, I *am* happy, really. I'm just happy *and*...something else."

Alky cut his eyes back at Depression. Depression gave a deep sigh.

"Hell—I can't remember the last time somebody made me feel like this." He paused. "Okay—I *can* remember. But it's been...jeez...well, you know."

Alky offered himself up. Woody took a sip.

"Maybe I'm one of those people who just can't sustain a relationship. It's not that I don't *want* to. All the stuff at the beginning—the things I say, the looks, the touches, the whole romantic, passionate ball of wax—they're all absolutely real. Genuine. I mean them at the time."

He took a small hit off the smoke and tapped it gently against the lip of the ashtray.

"But I'm like a walking relationship disaster. If love was charted on a weather map, I'd be a tornado. See—the problem is that we don't think of the tornado as anything other than a terrible *thing*— a force—something that came and went and left a horrible mess behind. I mean, what if the tornado was just trying to reach down from the sky and pick a single rose from the ground to give to someone, and...look what happened? What if the tornado felt horrible about what happened? Ya know? But nobody wants to hear that. Nobody wants a tornado around. A tornado has no sustained relationships."

The cigarettes just lay there, quietly considering the idea. Alky fizzed, clearly unconvinced—almost like he wanted to raise a question. Depression cleared his throat to get Alky's attention, frowned, and shook his head in a subtle don't-go-there gesture. Alky looked away and softly hummed the first two bars of the Billy Joel song "Honesty."

"Oh, yeah—like *you're* one to talk," Woody snapped at him. "Best policy, my ass. Hey—I don't claim to be the best practitioner of truth. Who is? ... I am, I think, a good observer of and commentator upon it. I mean, Christ—I understand completely how a piano works; I just can't play it."

Alky rolled his ice cubes. Woody tapped ashes into the ashtray and pushed them around a little with the cherry tip of the cigarette.

"Think about it. Nowhere else in nature is Truth considered a morality issue, except among us human beings. It's a survival issue, plain and simple. A moth looks like a moth... unless it needs to look like something else so a fuckin' predator won't eat it. But it just doesn't *decide* to lie about who it is. Because we humans *decide* to lie or to tell the truth, suddenly it's a morality issue? I mean, some friend shows you a picture of her new baby and asks, 'Isn't he *beautiful*?' Do you tell her you've seen better looking *chimps*? Or is the lie the nobler reply? It's not a morality issue; it's a question of whether or not you want the relationship to survive. Truth's not really one of the pillars of morality; it's more like a non-load-bearing wall we throw up or tear down as appearances require. She doesn't love my fuckin' *name*; she loves *me*."

The *L* word caught them all off guard. They cast quick looks at each other. Woody could see the smirk forming on Alky's face. He grabbed the glass and downed it, then set the empty down on the table beside the pack of smokes with a let-that-be-a-lesson-to-you look.

"Don't fuck with me," he said to his two remaining companions. Then he lifted the glass to the waitress. When she came over, he handed her the glass.

"Same thing," he deadpanned to her. "But tell him to hold the smart-ass this time."

The waitress took the glass, but looked puzzled. Woody studied her face for just a moment, then reached into his bag of facial expressions, rummaged around just a bit, and offered her a half-drunken smile. She relaxed and smiled back and turned to leave.

"Ya see?" he said to the smokes, and he pulled another one from the pack. "Whatever works."

Chapter 59

Casey sat in his car and looked at the small strip of efficiency apartments known as the Gull Cottages. They were of concrete construction, old, and painted swimming pool aqua. According to the address from the South Carolina DMV record, Donald R. Black's residence was the unit on the far right end of the sad, little, adjoined lodgings.

In front of the unit beside Donald R. Black's, a weary-looking Big Wheel tricycle lay on its side. In the small, gravel parking lot, there was one other car—a dusty brown Nissan with a yellow door on the driver's side—and a moped.

Casey got out of the car, walked to the gray-painted door of Donald Black's humble digs, and knocked. It was two o'clock in the afternoon. He didn't know whether to expect him to be home or not. When there was no answer, he knocked again. The door to the apartment next door opened, just wide enough for a little girl, about five years old, to fill the gap. The child looked Casey up and down for several seconds before she spoke.

"Mister Blackie's not there," she said and looked at him as if the information she had just imparted was a matter of common knowledge.

"Do you know where he is?" Casey asked. He smiled and knelt down to get on her level.

The child spoke as if explaining it to a developmentally-challenged playmate. "He went home to be with the angels."

Before Casey could react, the door opened wider, and a pregnant young woman with corn-rowed blonde hair and a nose ring stood behind the little girl.

"Boy, she's somethin', id'n she? Never met a stranger."

"I'm..." Casey stood up and quickly tried to re-group. "I'm looking for Donald R. Black."

"Oh, yeah?" She cocked her head. "You a bill collector or a salesman? You ain't friend or fam'ly, or you'd already know he's—" she paused and looked down at the little girl, then back up, "—gone to live with the angels."

"I'm...neither. I'm—oh—" he stopped and introduced himself and explained that he was working on a missing persons case.

"Well, he ain't missin'. They know right where he's at. You didn't know him at all?"

"No. Unfortunately, we never met," Casey replied. He was completely sincere about the *unfortunately* part.

"Boy, I'll tell you—he was a trip without luggage. Sad thing, what happened. Hirie can prob'ly tell you a whole lot more'n I can, though, about it. You talk to him yet?" She stopped and rolled her eyes. "No—I guess not or else you'da already known about Blackie, wouldn't you? I don't know what's wrong with me sometimes. Nothin' a few days of free twenty-four hour child care wouldn't cure, if you know what I mean."

"Can you tell me where I might find this
226

Hirie you mentioned?" Casey looked down at the little girl, who had grabbed him by the legs and was now standing with her feet on the tops of his feet.

"Now, Denise—he don't wanna dance with you right now. You get off that man's feet." The young woman reached forward and plucked the child from Casey, swiveled, and set her down just inside their front door. "We'll dance later," she said to the girl, then turned back to Casey. "Don't pay her any attention. We do that sometime when the radio's playin', so she thinks ever'body does it. Like I said, she never met a stranger."

"No—that's fine." Casey realized he was kind of mumbling. He cleared his throat. "So...this Hirie..." he prompted.

"Oh! Right. He's prob'ly up at the station, I imagine."

"The station?"

"The service station. Hirie's Exxon? That's where Blackie worked. You passed it right back up there on the main drag—" she pointed back in the direction of the larger road that Casey had come in on, "—right before you turned to come down here, I bet."

Casey thanked her and turned to go back to his car. He stopped, as if he'd forgotten something, and looked back at the door. The little girl was standing in the doorway, waving to him. He waved back.

"Bye, Denise," he called. "Thank you for the dance."

Chapter 60

It didn't take long for Tony Bozzone and
partners Dorothy Thorn and Randall Ring to hook
up. Even in a city the size of New York, it doesn't
take Hercule Poirot to figure out that, if you've got
one man clutching a knife with a broken blade and
another man with a broken knife blade stuck in his
leg, the two men may have shared a moment at
some time in their lives. What it does take is
attention to detail, documentation that can withstand
the closest legal scrutiny, and the ability to articulate
how it at all comes together and what it adds up to.

Within a couple of days, the three detectives
were sitting together and comparing notes. Bozzone
primarily had the tip of the knife blade from Jock
Dejohnette's leg, of course. He also voiced his
concerns about the credibility of his "victim's"
account of his assault. The shirt and pants, too, were
key items of evidence. The pants definitely had
Dejohnette's blood on them. Both the pants and the
shirt could be tested for traces of someone else's
blood. Bozzone wished he had seized the black tote
bag, as well.

The crime scene that Thorn and Ring had
inherited was a cornucopia of forensic goodies.
They had an eye witness. Unfortunately, Shane
Callahan's vision of what the suspect looked like
was clouded by fire and blood and dog shit,
darkness and panic and shock. And that was just for
starters. It yielded little more than a vague

description of a medium-sized white male. The detectives hoped that, if they could put together a physical line-up, the suspect's face would leap out at Callahan through all the lingering distractions. But a line-up meant having a suspect in custody to include in that procedure. Taking the suspect into custody meant putting together articulable probable cause to get an arrest warrant. There were shell casings and fatal bullets, but there was, as yet, no gun to match them to. Finding the gun would likely require a search warrant, and that required its own set of articulable legal probabilities. There were, so far, no usable fingerprints from the scene. Even if there were, they, too, needed a suspect to link them to the incident. No—their best witness right now was Blackie Black—Donald R. Black, according to his South Carolina driver's license—and the silent testimony he and his broken Barlow could provide.

There was vital DNA evidence, to be sure, but even marked "RUSH," they knew the DNA comparative analysis results were weeks away. So, what they turned to was the forensic reunion of blade tip to broken Barlow. They needed to show that the two pieces, not only fit together, but that they had been one, at one time.

Comparative micrography is the science of assembling microscopic puzzles. It uses methods similar to the ones used in ballistics comparisons and toolmark examinations. Essentially, it matches striations and grain, and in a case such as this one, precisely fits one puzzle piece to another.

Step two—establishing that the pieces not only fit, but were, in fact, once one piece requires the use of a gas chromatographer-mass spectrometer (GC-MS). A knife blade is the end product of a process that begins with a specific recipe of metallic soup and ends with tempering and polishing procedures that, together, yield a unique, identifiable, metallic compound which, if separated into pieces, can be matched by analyzing minute samples of each piece on a molecular level. Samples are vaporized, fragmented, and filtered. Identification of a compound rests on the premise that every compound has a unique fragmentation pattern.

Just about the time that little Denise was fitting the bottoms of her bare feet to the tops of Casey Frye's shoes for a slow dance under the eaves of the Gull Cottages in Myrtle Beach, a technician in New York was finalizing his report of how he had fitted the tip of the knife blade from Jock Dejohnette's left femur to the broken blade of the Barlow knife found clutched in Blackie Black's right hand.

Chapter 61

"I thought the world of him an' all, and if there was a better mechanic anywhere, I don't know who it is, but I'll just tell you the God's truth, I ain't got that kinda money." Hirie Meeks paused and wiped his face with a faded red rag. "I mean, I feel *bad.* I've lost sleep—you can ask my wife—and hell, she feels as bad as I do—but you got any idea what they charge to send a body all the way back down here? And they won't do it at all 'til they do the embalmin' an' all up there first. At New York prices is what I'm talkin' about! I'm serious—it's the damndest thing I ever tried to figure out in my whole life. Like I said, I thought the world an' all of Blackie, but this is somethin' fam'ly us'lly's s'posed to take care of, id'n it? I don't know what's gonna happen, but I jus' don't know what I can do about it."

"And he never mentioned any family?" Casey asked.

"Not to me, he didn't. Not to anybody else I know of."

It had been three days since the Myrtle Beach police had come by and informed Hirie Meeks of the bizarre murder of Blackie Black. Casey wasn't sure how long they would hold the body up in New York before they consigned Blackie Black to a pauper's grave.

From the description that he got of Blackie

Black from Hirie Meeks, Casey was fairly certain that the man Hirie described was *not* the same man who had enchanted his mother and who had switched identities with Don Black. But, based on Hirie's payroll records of Blackie, it was equally clear that the man who had been known around there as Blackie Black was using the same name, date of birth, and social security number as the man Casey sought. Casey thought it was the oddest incongruity he had ever encountered. Then Mimi Meeks arrived.

As she stepped from her car, Casey's eyes were drawn instantly to her long, incredibly well-turned legs. He followed the remarkable curves of her body all the way up to her face. It was not unlike driving along an exquisitely beautiful winding country road, only to arrive at the county landfill. It took him a moment to hit the "clear" and "reset" buttons in his brain. Mimi Meeks didn't seem to notice.

She only had one noteworthy bit of new information to offer. Blackie had a tattoo on his left upper arm which read: *U.S.S. Wren*. She had noticed it once when Blackie had changed his shirt at the station.

"Were you a sailor, Mr. Black?" she had asked him.

"Oh," he had replied and then swatted at the tattoo like he was trying to shoo it away. "Yeah," he had said, finally, "but I'm not supposed to talk about it."

She thought Blackie might have been part of some elite, top secret, naval strike force. Neither Casey nor Hirie saw any sense in trying to point out to her how unlikely that was.

Chapter 62

Jock Dejohnette could feel the law closing in on him. At times, it was as if he could hear the click of pieces of the case being fitted together. He had hardly slept at all since that night. Day One had merely been irksome—the debacle replaying itself over and over in his head; then the story in the *Post*—the way they portrayed him: *Hooded Freak Spreads Death and Dog Poop in Brooklyn.*

There was no mention of him as a suspect, of course. But the story did say that the dead hayseed may have wounded his attacker with a knife. The detective at the hospital had surely read the story, he felt.

He thought about how, in old black and white movies, guys who had gotten themselves shot or stabbed and who couldn't risk the police finding out always knew some old drunk who used to be a doctor but who had had his license lifted because of some botched operation that had left a budding young piano virtuoso paralyzed or some such shit, but who would patch them up with shaky hands in exchange for a bottle of rotgut whiskey; they always knew some sleazy photographer for a cheap girlie magazine who moonlighted in manufacturing fake passports and identity papers for guys on the lam. Where *were* these shadowy underworld characters when you really needed them?

Where could he go? Who could he get to hide him until he could figure out how to disappear?

Where could he stash his stuff? He glanced around his apartment. If you have to grab just a few things and run, what do you take? Certainly, his laptop with all of his work, his files. Some clothes. The Savage. He almost laughed when he looked at the stacks of unsold copies of earlier *Retributor* issues and the tee-shirts. The story in the *Post* had touched on the curious message scrawled on the "Curb Your Dog" sign. Too late to worry about the comics and the shirts. If the police made it as far as his apartment, they would have already connected the lightning-bolt *R* with his comic book alter-ego. No—he just needed a place to lie low, think, and plan his new life.

His sister, Marie, came to mind. He hadn't seen her in years. Hadn't even talked to her. After his dad died, his mother had re-married. Sid. A meat-cutter at a Key Food supermarket. Then his mother had died. Breast cancer. Marie tried to stay in touch for a few years, but they didn't really know each other anymore. She married some jerk who worked for the MTA, and they moved to Queens. He and his sister had only seen each other at Christmas, when they gave each other gifts, each of which puzzled the other. She tended toward the gift of books. They weren't even best-sellers or publications that hinted at broad public appeal. He always gave her a jewelry box. He wasn't sure why.

One year she gave him *The Wit and Whimsy of Washington Irving*. Another year, it was *Best Loved Christmas Carols and the Stories Behind*

Them. The last year they had gotten together, she gave him a coffee table book, *Dogs of the Caribbean*.

"I thought you liked dogs," she'd said, "and remember how Mom always wanted to go down to the islands one day?"

She unwrapped her gift. The last words his sister had spoken to him—what had it been, five, six years?—were: "How much jewelry do you think I have?"

Chapter 63

The tattoo on Blackie Black's upper left arm had been routinely noted on the autopsy report for Donald R. Black, male Caucasian. It just hadn't set off any alarms or prompted any inquiry because, after all, the victim's wallet had contained all of the appropriate identification. The biggest problem that the Medical Examiner's office faced was the apparent lack of any next of kin or friends to take responsibility for the deceased's final arrangements.

Typically, the City of New York Medical Examiner's office will hold an unclaimed body for two weeks. A little longer, perhaps, in an unusual case, like this homicide.

In the case of some unfortunate indigent individual who dies of natural causes between the stenciled sheets of a hospital bed provided at taxpayers' expense, that individual often is afforded an opportunity that life's circumstances denied him when he could have really used it. He gets to go to medical school.

The bad news is that it is much like the bad joke Hannibal Lector makes when he says, "I'm having an old friend for dinner."

By law, medical schools in New York get first dibs on the fallen comrades of the Squeegee Brigade. An autopsy, however, renders the earthly remains of a forgotten ticketholder, stranded on the Stygian shore, unfit for cadaver duties within the Ivy halls where Hippocrates' apprentices come to play.

Blackie Black was on track for a dirt nap in Potter's Field. But he wasn't going anywhere for a couple of weeks. Luckily, that left his social calendar open for visitors, because Casey Frye was headed north already.

Chapter 64

Detectives Dorothy Thorn and Randall Ring prided themselves—individually, and as a team—on their attention to detail. They didn't like it when someone second-guessed their thoroughness. They especially didn't like it when that someone was little more than a rookie cop from a Podunk town in Virginia.

There had been no reason to even suspect that the body in the morgue was anyone other than exactly who the identification presented him to be. The inquiries through the Myrtle Beach Police Department—complete with an email-attached, close-up photo of Blackie in pre-autopsy repose—had confirmed who he was and had even shed light on what he was doing there.

Though they had rolled post-mortem fingerprints, a criminal history check had revealed no arrest record anywhere for this Donald R. Black. Therefore, there were no fingerprints in the FBI's criminal file against which to match the ones they had taken, anyway. It was cut-and-dried: Donald R. Black was simply a solid, if somewhat backwoods, citizen whose one bite of the Big Apple had been into a rotten spot. And now, here was this latter-day Barney Fife suggesting that their front-runner for in-court-sympathy-grabbing-poor-victim-of-senseless-violence dead-guy-of-the-month had lied on his application?! Casey was increasingly feeling like a batboy offering batting tips to Barry Bonds.

On the way there, Casey had considered trying to bullshit his way into whatever information the NYPD might have about Blackie Black. He knew that if he went with the story about investigating a missing persons case, Chief Singleton would back him up, if it came to that, but he really didn't want to put the Chief in the position of having to "bend the truth" on his account.

Instead, he apologized to Thorn and Ring for getting off on the wrong foot—for seeming to question their methods or their progress. Then he told them the truth. Mostly.

They had been all prepared to pop him on his young ass with a towel and send him scurrying from the locker room. They weren't prepared for him to play the officer-needs-assistance card.

He told them that he had cancer and that he was trying to find his biological father, in hopes of securing a transplant. He just didn't tell them what *kind* of transplant. He left it to their individual imaginations to fill in the blanks about which organ the Big C had a strangle-hold on.

He told them about the tattoo. In addition to the forty-some-odd million fingerprint records that the FBI has in its criminal file, they maintain thirty-something million cards in their civil file—mostly fingerprint records of those who are serving or who have served in the armed forces.

Thorn and Ring said they would request a check of Blackie Black's prints against those civil files. It might take a while, they told him. Get a room. See the sights. Catch a show. *Proof*, maybe.

Chapter 65

Casey Frye slid his mother's credit card across the check-in counter to the clerk—Vince, according to his name badge—at the Arlington Hotel. He would sort out his motives later, he thought, as Vince collected an imprint of the card; right now, he just needed a room. Detectives Thorn and Ring had not made a point of telling him that Blackie Black had been staying at the Arlington. It was just mentioned in their re-cap of what they had put together on the case.

Casey wasn't shopping for a New York hotel. There was no trying to decide between the brilliant chrome bustle and rush of the Marriott Marquis with its towering neon view and the intimate charm and quiet elegance of the Iroquois. He just needed a place to lay his head. If he had checked with a travel agent about tourist-class hotels in New York, the agent would have winked and nodded, as if letting him in on an insider's secret, and would have said of the Arlington, "Great rooms. Great rates."

The fact that the late Blackie Black had stayed there provided, in some odd way, a tiny beacon of purpose in a nearly overwhelming sea of humanity at its most distracting. He had already decided he would probably *not* see the sights, *not* catch a show. Maybe if he were here under different circumstances—with Debbie, perhaps—but not this time.

"I, uh, had a friend who stayed here recently," Casey heard himself say to Vince. "Donald Black. From South Carolina?" He paused, waiting for it to register with Vince that he was talking about the guest of the hotel who was just *murdered* a few days ago.

"Oh, yeah?" Vince replied, "That's where Myrtle Beach is, right?"

"Yeah. In fact, my friend was *from* Myrtle Beach." Again he paused and waited for the clerk to put it together.

"I been there one time. Golf package thing. Went to this big strip bar. You ever been there?" Casey wasn't sure if he meant the strip bar or Myrtle Beach. While he was deciding, Vince forged ahead. "Jesus. Spent a fortune."

"I was wondering," Casey inserted quickly, "if it'd be possible to get the same room my friend stayed in." Casey wasn't sure why he was asking. It wasn't as if he had known Blackie Black. He didn't expect to find anything in the room that would shed any light on what had happened. "Donald R. Black," he continued. "He checked in last week."

"I don't know," Vince said. "Lemme look." He tapped around on the keyboard of the computer for a minute. Paused. Tapped some more. "Yeah," he said, finally, "810. How many nights?"

"Two," Casey told him. "It might turn out to be longer. I'll let you know."

"No problem," Vince said. He hit a key on the computer, and the new check-in form began printing.

He never even made the connection, Casey thought.

"So..." Vince pushed the form over to Casey for his signature. He pointed to a line marked by a small x. "...you gonna see the sights?"

"I, uh..." Casey signed his name. *A man checks in, stays at their hotel, gets shot down in the street, and no one here even remembers?!* "...I don't think so."

What he could really use right now was a refuge from a city that ate guileless visitors like Blackie Black—*and himself?* he wondered—for midnight snacks.

Chapter 66

New Yorkers keep about two million dogs and cats as pets in their homes. No one is really willing to even venture a guess as to the number of strays, but the City manages to round-up fifty or sixty thousand a year. If you give them credit for nabbing ten percent of the critters...well, run the numbers. They catch a lot more dogs than cats.

When it comes to stray people, on any given day in the city, the homeless population is around 35,000. To put that into perspective, that is roughly, and ironically, the size of *Homestead*, Florida. Or Rome, Georgia—which, oddly enough, and perhaps just to make a point, may *have* been built in a day. A Saturday, in December, 1834. Or, if they all got on a giant bus, and headed up to Maine, and got off, and all squatted in one place, they would, in one day, become that state's second largest city.

Dogs—bless their domesticated little hearts and social proclivities—if turned out onto the streets, will by and large turn into beggars. They may scavenge a little. Oh, after several generations, if they have some open spaces and some sort of food chain where they can break in line, they will form themselves into hunting packs. But...a dog, on his own, without a little luck, will starve to death.

A cat, on the other hand, left on his own, will turn feral over a long weekend, if you don't watch out. He will revert to predator, tell the CEO of Fancy Feast gourmet pet vittles to kiss his tabby ass, and go kill something for dinner.

Among the homeless of the homo sapiens ilk, most are dogs. A few are cats. As Jock Dejohnette gathered his essentials and prepared to lose himself for a while among the NYC street folks, he was sure he would be a cat.

Chapter 67

Tony Bozzone was about as computer savvy as a man his age ought to be, he figured. He could do pretty much all of the job-related inquiries and entries that modern law enforcement demanded. He owned his own laptop and had his own email address. He could surf the web, though he couldn't build a website. He knew what a hacker was, but he wouldn't know where to begin if he wanted to hack into a site himself. He wasn't above looking at a little porn on the web, but he'd never had cybersex—didn't understand it; didn't see the attraction. He didn't appreciate the intrusion of "penis enhancement" spam, but he had made some on-line purchases—Amazon.com and ProFlowers.com—last Mother's Day.

He had clicked around the various law enforcement databases, looking for Jock Dejohnette, and had found very little. One stolen bicycle report in which Dejohnette was listed as the complainant, nearly two years ago. Different address, though, from the one he'd provided at the hospital. The address he had listed at the hospital had turned out to be fake, it seemed. Bozzone had checked it out, discreetly. It was a legitimate address, but the apartment there was occupied by a tall blonde running enthusiast and his slim, gay, Latino lover. No sign of Jock Dejohnette.

Bozzone typed "Jock Dejohnette" into the window at Google and sent it spinning off into cyberspace. In approximately .11 seconds, the Google fairy served him up the connection to an e-zine website for *The Retributor*. A few clicks of the mouse later, Detective Bozzone echoed the exclamation of an earlier comic hero: *Shazam!* He was looking at the red thunderbolt *R* from the back of the "Curb Your Dog" sign. He decided it might be time to get to know more about the adventures of Dejohnette's black-clad urban avenger.

Chapter 68

Two things get you caught, Jock reasoned. *Stupidity and bad luck.*

He had run into a little bad luck with the way the last civil action had gone. No way to have foreseen that. But the bad luck was more the hayseed's than his. He hadn't been caught. Now, luck was actually on his side, he figured. Or the odds, at least, were in his favor. He was one face in a crowd of eight million. It wasn't like he had shot the President or anything. There would be no massive manhunt. No dragnet. For a moment, he heard in his head the theme song from the old Jack Webb series. He'd only seen it in re-runs on TVLand.

Serial killers get away with it for years, he thought. *While they continue to kill, even!* They keep pushing their luck. And that's just stupid. He was smarter than that, and luck was with him. He had a plan.

He would simply disappear. Leave New York. Assume a new identity in a new city. He needed some traveling money and the seeds of a new identity. If planned and carried out correctly, it would require one more bold act. Just one. And then a rather routine pilfering of a few purses. That part was no problem. He had it down to an art form.

For years, Jock had worked through several temp services. Before he abandoned his apartment, he'd had the presence of mind to take along a manila envelope with time sheets from a few of the temporary services. When one of the services called and offered him an assignment, if he was at that point when he had to lower himself to play day-worker, he simply showed up at the designated office. He presented a time sheet—three carbonless copies, usually—to some insipid "human resources" lackey, then waded off into the pool of glum-faced office drones.

He had decided on K.O.L. Temps, a service that had sent him out a few times in the past, all inconspicuous, mindless, lost-amongst-the-herd kinds of assignments. The company name was kind of an inside joke. The temp service was actually a fairly clever solution to the problem of finding summer employment for two college roommates—Kim Shapiro and Larry Farber—from Long Island University back in the early 80s. They printed up some flyers, got themselves a telephone listing, and offered day workers to various offices in lower Manhattan for the summer. Their only problem was that, for that first summer, they only had two workers to offer: Kim or Larry. Thus, the Kim or Larry Temporary Service was launched—K.O.L. Now, K.O.L. handled some of the biggest temp jobs in lower Manhattan—sometimes sending out nearly a hundred workers a day to a single company. Jock had a couple of their time sheets. Not that he would ever collect a paycheck from them for this job. The time sheet would simply be his ticket into the pool. In an hour or so, he would have tapped all the purses he needed and be gone. It would be his last few hours in New York—a quick harvest of travel funds on his way out of town.

That part would be a cinch. There was, however, one bold act that had to precede the harvest, and it had to be just perfect.

He would pick out a tourist. It had to be a man—one who at least vaguely resembled himself. Someone whose driver's license he could pass off as his own. It was a shame, he thought, that men didn't carry purses like women. A snatch-and-run would be so much easier to do. And less risky. But no—men carried wallets, and they didn't give them up willingly. This was going to require a genuine, old-fashioned stick-up. Show the man the gun; grab the wallet; make the getaway.

With any luck, the wallet would contain a driver's license, social security card, credit cards, maybe. The credit cards would almost certainly be canceled immediately. That was okay. He didn't need them primarily for their purchasing power.

Once he had these items, he would find a nice, out-of-the-way, medium-sized city. Somewhere in the mid-west, maybe. He would find a little place to rent, cheap. Get a phone or a utility bill in his new name. A pay stub from some piss-ant job. He would find a DMV office—just busy enough so he didn't stand out. He would tell them he recently moved there, show them his proof of residency, and turn in his old, out-of-state driver's license for a brand new one with his very own picture on it. After that, he was free to go wherever he wanted—wrap himself in his new identity and start over.

The key, of course, was finding the right tourist. Follow him. Plan it out. It had to go down exactly right. Another dead tourist would attract all the wrong kind of attention.

Chapter 69

Over the Christmas holidays, during his sophomore year, 1989, Andy Miller gave his mother a peach-colored sweater and broke her heart. He had come home to Springfield, Ohio to tell her that he was dropping out of Cedarville College and that he was gay.

It had been a year for heartbreak in the Miller house. It was the family's first Christmas without Andy's father, Doug. Doug had been the victim of International Harvester's only fatal industrial accident that year. A shelf had collapsed in the warehouse where Doug worked, and a crate of combine parts had crushed him. Secretly, one of his co-workers with a bent for morbid humor later suggested an ad campaign touting: *Even the Grim Reaper Prefers International Harvester!*

If his father had lived, there's no telling when, if ever, Andy might have come out of the closet. Virtually every move that Andy had made in his young life up to that point had been plotted against the latitude of "What will Dad think?" and the longitude of "What will Dad say?" Andy had gone away to Cedarville College because: (1) It was a "good Christian school" and (2) Doug Miller had pitched for the Cedarville Yellow Jackets baseball team, including the 1966 team which won the Mid-Ohio Conference Championship.

Doug Miller had passed along to Andy, and almost obsessively nurtured within him, one remarkable talent: the ability to throw a 92 MPH four-seam fastball to virtually any point where a catcher chose to hold his mitt. Andy wrapped himself in the sports obsession to help explain his lack of interest in the opposite sex. His dad liked to say, "It's okay. He's *focused*. There'll be plenty of time for girls later."

When Andy broke the news to his mother, his bags were already packed and loaded in his old Toyota Corolla. He was moving to Cleveland, he told her, to study hair styling. He also mentioned his undying love for the Cleveland Indians.

His mother cried. He told her that she would always be the only woman he ever loved. His younger sister Margaret said it was "gross." He turned to her and added, "...and you'll be the only *girl*."

Nearly twelve years later, Andy Miller was quite the in-demand stylist in Cleveland, his fastball had lost not one smidgen of its zing, and he was off to New York for a week as a guest instructor at the Redken Exchange. Lady Fortuna was smiling on Andy Miller, it seemed. However, being the capricious enigma that she is—if Fortuna *has* motives, they are certainly unfathomable—one might wonder if she *thought* she was smiling at Jock Dejohnette. Because Andy Miller did bear a striking resemblance to Jock Dejohnette.

Chapter 70

Dorothy Thorn sat staring at the FBI report in her hand. Something about the name was ringing a bell in her head; she just couldn't quite lock in on it.

"What is it?" her partner asked.

She didn't even look at Ring. She held up her hand, palm open towards him, and closed her eyes. He had seen the gesture before. He settled back in his own chair.

After a moment, she opened her eyes, stood up, and started to walk away.

"Where you going?" Ring asked.

She thrust the FBI report on the fingerprint check they had requested towards him, and said, "Evidence room."

Randall Ring looked at the report as she walked away. "Zildjian?" he called to her.

"Yeah," she called back, just before she turned the corner.

"Like the cymbal?" he said, to no one in particular.

After she signed for the bag, she took it from the evidence custodian, opened it, and took out the Barlow knife. She turned it over and looked at the name engraved on the backstrap. Zildjian. She smiled, pleased with herself that she had made the connection before her partner. Maybe she'd let him call the Barney with the cancer problem.

"It's odd, isn't it." It was a statement, not a question. Tony Bozzone raised his eyebrows a notch and nodded at the several sheets of stapled papers Casey held in his hand. Thorn had passed the report along to Bozzone to pass along to Casey.

"Yeah," Casey replied. "Can I keep these?"

"Yeah. I made you those copies," Bozzone said. "For what they're worth," he added.

"Does look like kind of a dead end." Casey looked back at the papers, just in case his eyes gave away what he was thinking. Which was that it was not a dead end at all. At least not for his purposes. He felt a little bad for what he was thinking: that if Clifford Woodrow Zildjian was anywhere to be found, *he* wanted to get to him before the NYPD.

To the New York detectives working the Blackie Black homicide, the peeling away of the Donald R. Black facade to reveal the musty, abandoned Clifford Woodrow Zildjian underneath was a bothersome and unwelcome complication. At the very least, it blemished the picture of Blackie Black as a down-home innocent, if the case ever went before a jury. In their minds, you didn't adopt a new identity unless you had something to hide— unless you were running from something, maybe. A spotless criminal record and nothing to indicate that the late C.W. Zildjian was any sort of fugitive only made things all the more untidy and curious.

"We're checking with the Marshal Service to see if there's any kind of witness protection program kind of deal, maybe."

"Maybe it's something as simple as disappearing from a former wife or something. The old 'I'm goin' out for a pack of cigarettes' and never came back thing," Casey suggested, though he knew better.

"No missing person report," the detective shook his head. "At least not that we've found."

"Yeah, but it'd have to be, what—eight or ten years ago? Some small town, maybe. Who knows what might've happened to a report like that?"

"That's true," Bozzone gave a little puff of disgust. "It's still a shitty little mess to leave behind if you're gonna go out and get yourself killed."

"I guess."

"Doesn't really do you much good, either, huh?"

"Well, it tells me he wasn't the guy I was looking for, I suppose."

"So what'll you do?"

"Go look for another Donald R. Black, I reckon."

Clifford Woodrow Zildjian, AKA Donald R. Black, was a dead man, according to the NYPD files. To Casey Frye, though, Clifford Woodrow Zildjian was a very much alive figure in the distance. He had shape-shifted. Again. But he hadn't disappeared.

In the bedroom of Merilee Mikatitis' Brooklyn apartment, she collapsed on top of

Woody, then rolled over beside him. His penis slipped from the hot buttered clasp of her vagina, and they both groaned.

"I feel like I've died and gone to heaven," she sighed.

"Me, too," Woody whispered.

Chapter 71

Redken would pick up the tab for the room at the Marriott Marquis for seven nights. Andy Miller had decided he would fly in a day early. He flew out of Cleveland's Hopkins International Airport on Saturday morning. He had already called a friend who worked at Josephina's across from Lincoln Center to arrange dinner there Saturday night, late. He waited around 'til Chad got off work at the restaurant, then spent the night at his place. He was meeting the folks from Redken for lunch on Sunday. He would see if he could check in early at the Marriott.

He was a little relieved that he had the lunch meeting as an excuse to not invite Chad to come with him to the hotel. He felt only a little guilty. Chad had been so nice to let him stay there. Dinner had been lovely. The sex had been merely okay. It was "thank you" sex. And it was "thank you" enough, really, he thought. He kept the idea of a luxurious room overlooking the lights of Broadway...all by him...unless he *chose* to invite someone up...a new friend, perhaps...tucked away like an individually wrapped sweet.

There was something about pulling up to the front of the hotel in a taxi—the solid "chunk" sound of a car door being closed, echoing through the covered, ground floor, drive-through colonnade— that made him feel like a visiting dignitary. It was a feeling he would like to have the opportunity to get used to, he thought to himself.

As his luggage was being passed from the cabbie to the bellhop, Andy reached into the front pocket of his houndstooth trousers where he kept his small bills, in order of denomination, all facing the same way, ones on top, folded over once, and snugged in a gold-plated money clip with his initials on it. He didn't notice the man standing beside one of the large slate-gray columns, a short distance away. Jock Dejohnette noticed him, though.

Chapter 72

Sunday night, Casey hardly slept at all after Chief Clarence Singleton called him back with the information on Clifford Woodrow Zildjian. Casey had figured he might end up having to drive back down south. To the Carolinas, or maybe even to Florida. And that was if he was lucky. If Chief Singleton could turn something up. He figured he would go back home for a day or two before he continued his search. And then Chief Singleton called. There was a Clifford Woodrow Zildjian right there in New York. In Brooklyn.

Casey felt a little guilty about not sharing the information with the detectives at NYPD, especially Detective Bozzone—he was a pretty good guy, and seemed to actually give a shit—but he was glad he had trusted his instinct to not question them about whether they'd done a simple driver's license check. They seemed to believe that Clifford Woodrow Zildjian was a name that Blackie Black had simply discarded, sloughed off like an old skin and abandoned, for reasons they had yet to discover. They assumed Blackie has tossed the identity into the trash can, so they had no reason to check in the recycle bin.

It was late when he called Debbie. He could tell by her hello that he had awakened her.

"I'm sorry," he said. "I know it's late."

"No—it's okay. It's more than okay. I'm glad you called. I've been worried."

"I'm sorry to worry you."

"Stop saying you're sorry. ... Say you're glad. To hear my voice."

"I'm glad to hear your voice."

"I'm glad you're glad."

"I talked to Chief Singleton tonight. He had some news for me."

"What kind of news? Good news, I hope."

"That's just it, Deb. I don't know any more."

"Don't know what, Casey?"

"It's turned into this...game, almost. Hide and seek. I don't know how much longer I want to play."

"Come home, Casey. Just pack up and come back home."

"I will. After I check out this one last thing. If this turns out to be nothing...or another screwed-up deal like the others...I think I'm done with it. ... Deb...I need to ask you something."

"What is it?"

"Can you be married to a man who can't give you children?"

"Casey—I love you."

"And I love you, but that wasn't the question. Can you? If none of this works out...if it turns out it's just going to be you and me and that's it...our whole lives...could you do that?"

"Yes."

"You didn't even *think* about it, Debbie, for God's sake! I'm *serious*."

"I don't *have* to think about it, Casey. I *have*

thought about it. ... You think you're the only one who's going through this?! ... I'm sorry. I know it's your body, and I know it has to be harder on you than on the rest of us, but you're not alone in this, Casey. You're not."

"I'm sorry. Don't...I didn't call to make you cry."

"... I'd rather cry with you than go to Disneyworld with Brad Pitt."

"Is he still calling? I oughta kick his Hollywood ass. ... Was that a laugh or a hiccup?"

"A little of both. ... When are you coming home?"

"Soon. I have to check out one last thing tomorrow. In Brooklyn. One more name. Either way, then, I'm coming home."

"I miss you, Casey."

"I miss you, too, baby. ... Get some sleep. I'll call you tomorrow."

"I don't want to hang up. I want to lie here and just listen to your voice...listen to you breathing 'til I fall asleep. Why doesn't somebody invent a phone that'll hang itself up when you fall asleep?"

"I'll start working on that as soon as I get back."

"When you get back, I won't need it."

"Good night, baby. Sweet dreams."

"You, too. ... 'Night."

If Debbie dreamed at all that night, she didn't remember it in the morning. Casey dreamed he was in an operating room, lying on an operating table. There was another operating table parallel to his, a few feet away. Dr. Strejc stood between the two tables, masked, gowned and gloved. Casey couldn't see the face of the person on the other table. Dr. Strejc was in the way, bent over the other patient. Suddenly, he straightened up, pulled his mask off, and threw it to the floor. "This man *has* no balls!" he said. "Don't you think somebody might've noticed that before you wheeled him in here?!" Casey woke up. He didn't get much sleep the rest of the night.

Chapter 73

It was a simple matter, finding out his name and room number. Jock Dejohnette simply picked up his own suitcase, followed Andy Miller inside, and stood behind him at the check-in counter. Just before Andy's check-in was completed and it was to be his turn, Jock feigned seeing someone he was supposed to meet and told the couple behind him to go ahead. He hurried away, as if to catch someone just leaving, all the while silently repeating to himself, "Miller. 1803. Miller. 1803. ...."

For several days he had caught naps where he could get them. During the day, he would nap like a weary traveler with his suitcase, in one of the waiting areas at Grand Central or the LIRR. At night, when the cars were nearly empty, he would ride the A train and snooze from Washington Heights to Aqueduct and back again. He had gotten sponge bathing and shaving down to a science in the restrooms of hotel mezzanines and McDonald's. A quick change of tee-shirt, and he was good to go. The leg still throbbed some and slowed him down more than he liked. But with the arrival of Mr. Miller, Room 1803, things were looking up. The pieces of the plan were coming together nicely. With a little luck, he would be on his way tomorrow. Then he could relax.

I can pass for this Miller guy, he thought. Except for the hair. He didn't like the short spiky coif Miller wore. He was already fairly certain of the man's sexual orientation. *Faggot*, he thought. Of course, that worked to his advantage, he figured. In Jock's mind, homosexuals were weak and made for easy prey. *He'll probably piss himself when I stick the gun in his face.*

Tomorrow had to be perfect. He would do it in Miller's room. Early. 8 o'clock. Knock on the door. Call him by name. That was one of the keys. By *name*. "Mr. Miller? This is John from the front desk." Offer up a name of your own. Sound official. Business-like. "I have a package for you that was left at the desk. They asked that it be delivered to you." Clearly, he was in town on business of some sort. Even if he wasn't expecting a package, he would *have* to open the door. Curiosity would compel him. And that's all he would need.

Push inside. Point the gun. Get his wallet. Get out of there. Down the stairs a few floors. Grab an elevator. Get outside. Head downtown. Maybe stop at a couple of jewelry stores along the way. See if the credit cards would fly. Small stuff. Easy to pawn later. An expensive watch. Diamond earrings. Report to the temp assignment. He knew just the place. Hit some purses for cash. Straight to Grand Central. And kiss this city goodbye.

It played out in his head as seamless as a Neil Simon script. Miller. Marriott. Monday. It couldn't miss.

Chapter 74

If one had been the epigrammatical fly on the wall during the cloistered moments shared by Woody and Merilee up until that point in their relationship, one may have marveled at—envied, even—the amount of their time together during which they were naked and either toying with the idea of, actually engaged in, or luxuriating in the afterglow of sex, which viewed through the panoramic scope of 4000 lenses in each compound eye would likely assume the proportions of IMAX porn. (IMAX is a registered trademark of the IMAX Corporation, which neither promotes nor condones cinematic depictions of two-stories-tall, womb-jelly-slickened penises plumbing the depths of glistening, pink-lipped, Lincoln-Tunnelesque twats.) The uncharacteristically serious shift in Woody's tone that Sunday evening, then, surely would have had any voyeuristic wall-crawler worth his suction cups creeping a bit farther down the vertical plane and tilting his antennae a little more in the direction of the conversation.

"How relaxed would you say you were right now—" he asked, "—a wet noodle, or lizard on a warm rock?"

She stretched and rubbed the top of her foot lazily up and down the side of his calf. It was just an excuse to run barefoot one more time through the plush pile bumblebee song that emanated from the bioluminescent fields of their own private aurora borealis.

"How 'bout a wet noodle on a warm rock?" she purred. She raised her arms above her head, causing her breasts to ride up a bit and wobble in a little understated dance of the pyramids. It was worth watching before he continued.

"I was having a little conversation the other day about things we haven't told each other— scratch that—about things I haven't told *you*, and something came up."

She was suddenly all ears, as they say— though other body parts may have argued the point very convincingly.

"Having a conversation with whom?"

"With myself."

"Ah. Those are always a treat. ... So, what did you say to yourself that you thought needed discussing?"

"How do you see yourself in, say, five years?"

"Are you saying you asked *yourself* that, or are you asking *me*?"

"I'm asking you."

"Why?"

"Because—and this is odd for me—I wonder if you see me anywhere in that picture."

She rolled over onto her side, facing him, and looked him in the eyes for several long moments.

"This is new," she said.

"Yes. It is. Or it's been so long that it feels

like new."

"This picture," she said, "would you *like* to be in it?"

"Yes," he whispered. It was almost a confession. "For an awfully long time, I've made a point to be in the here-and-now. To the extent that the past was like it never even happened, and the future was not something to even think about."

"And now it matters—this picture I'm supposed to have in my head?"

"This is hard to explain," he began. "I don't think I can talk about the future—if I'm in that picture, I mean—until I tell you about the past. And I'm afraid if I tell you about the past, we won't talk about the future, because I won't be in that picture anymore."

"This is like one of those things where you close your eyes and let yourself fall backwards, and you're supposed to learn how much trust you have in your partner to catch you."

"I never liked that game."

"You're a catcher. You've never had to be the faller, have you?"

"Not if I could help it," he said.

"Nobody can make you close your eyes and fall back, you know. Not even the one who's supposed to catch you."

"I know. I'm...I'm going to close my eyes now. I'm not going to fall backwards yet, but I'm going to close my eyes. While I've got my eyes closed, I'd like you to tell me about that picture.

Would you do that for me?"

"In the picture," she said softly, "There's me—" she paused, "—my hair is different—" He smiled. She smiled back, though he couldn't see it. "—and I see you..."

"How's my hair?" he asked.

"A little more gray," she answered. "Just along the temples. It's what you get for being such an old cradle-robber."

"It's what *you* get for being born so late, kiddo."

"It's okay—the gray, I mean. Makes you look 'distinguished'."

"Yeah. That would be me."

"And one other thing..."

"What?"

"Sometimes I see someone else. Small. Just learning to walk good."

He opened his eyes, and looked into hers. "I love you," he said.

"And I love you," she smiled. This time he saw it.

"And now I have a story to tell you," he sighed. "You might want to buckle your seatbelt for this."

Chapter 75

Andy Miller waited until after his lunch meeting on Sunday to unpack. He had arranged his hang-up clothes in the closet. Right to left. Jackets; shirts; trousers. In order of the day of the week he planned to wear them. He would need time, though, to arrange things in the dresser drawers and to lay out and organize his toiletries, so he set aside the entire afternoon for putting his room in order for the week. He had been careful in his selection of toiletry and personal grooming products so that Redken items were prominently displayed, in case the occasion should arise for him to entertain some dashing young Redken executive in his room.

His lunch hosts had been cordial, but all business. It was an entirely flirt-free environment. So far. They had mentioned some new products that he would get a chance to try out this week. He made reservations for dinner at seven at Sardi's. He was hoping for at least one celebrity sighting, just so that when he got back home he could say with practiced, piss-elegant casualness, "Well, dinner at Sardi's was absolutely divine, except—did you know Nathan Lane slurps his soup? I mean, when he talks, he does that thing with his eyes that is to *die* for, but the dear man *slurps* his soup!"

He would have liked to have gone down to the Village, but—no—not the night before his first day at the Exchange. He was to be there at nine. He left a request for a 7 a.m. wake-up call.

Jock found an all-night movie shoot going on outside the Port Authority Bus Terminal. There must have been two hundred extras, who were amassed between takes in a nearby church basement. Jack slipped in amongst one group returning from a scene, and he was pleased to see that the crowd was being used, it seemed, in shifts. Three groups. While one group was away, the members of the other two groups sat around and read and chatted, or lay around and napped. Jack got in four hours of decent snooze time. He even helped himself to a ham sandwich, a banana, and a Diet Pepsi before he wandered out with Group Two at nearly 4 a.m., then slipped away from the herd and headed for Times Square.

He had a pretty big production of his own to get ready for. And the curtain was going up in only a few hours.

Chapter 76

If you sit in a car, watching the front door of a place long enough, odds are that someone, eventually, will go in or come out. Unfortunately, if you sit in a car, watching the front door of a place long enough, a full bladder, eventually, will trump vigilant intentions.

Casey was parked across the street from the Renaissance Revival rowhouse that matched the address Clarence Singleton had given him on the phone. He had sat there for nearly three hours. He told himself that no one was home, that Clifford Woodrow Zildjian—*this* Clifford Woodrow Zildjian—would probably be at work, anyway. He didn't want to try to explain it all to anyone else who might answer the door. That's what he told himself. If he told himself that often enough and loudly enough, he couldn't hear that other voice inside him that asked, *You're not afraid to knock on that door, are you?*

He would watch. Until...something happened. He wasn't sure what.

The bladder and the superego element of the human psyche have enjoyed a long and fruitful relationship, dating back to prehistoric potty training. Cave drawings depict a sad-faced, clearly guilt-ridden Neanderthal toddler sitting in a puddle of pee upon an antelope hide. A Neanderthal mom stands nearby, arms akimbo, glowering at the young prehistoric ancestor of countless unborn bedwetters.

The eyes and the stomach long ago worked out a similar arrangement. In fact, no aspect of human physiology is as tight with the eyes as the stomach is, with the possible exception of the penis.

It was fairly easy, then, for the bladder to work a side deal wherein, if the eyes would underscore every bladder contraction with a move toward a likely bathroom-equipped eating establishment, once inside the establishment, the superego would launch into several verses of "You Can't Just Use the Restroom without Buying Something"—which was enjoying a revival on the country charts—thereby securing a tasty treat for Growlmaster Stō, as the stomach was currently billing himself in gastro-intestinal circles. After a quick consultation between the eyes and the stomach, the deal was struck: the pizza joint on the next corner.

Casey walked up to the counter inside and ordered a slice of pepperoni and a Pepsi, eyed the restroom, and told the guy behind the counter he'd be right back. Bladder took his own good time inside, enjoying the moment. When Casey returned to the counter, he handed the man a ten. As he waited for his change, he watched a large, hairy man wearing a black net tee-shirt fold his slice of pizza over and wolf down an enormous bite. *Weird*, Casey thought, *these people up here don't even know how to eat pizza.* As he stepped outside and took his own first bite, he felt the molten cheese plaster itself to the roof of his mouth and raise a blister there. After a rousing chorus of Ooos and Ahhhs with a distinctly simian ring to them, the fold-over suddenly made a lot of sense. He took a swig of Pepsi and traced the blister with the tip of his tongue as he started back to his car.

There is some obscure subsection of a statute somewhere in Code of Natural Law that dictates that if you are waiting for something to happen—the phone to ring; your team to score; your century plant to bloom—and you leave to go to the bathroom, that is the very time that the thing will occur.

Casey saw him come out of the front door of the rowhouse. He was undecided as to whether to try to run to catch him or not. He wasn't sure what to do with the pizza and drink. He looked around for a trash can. Growlmaster Stō churned in protest.

The man pointed his keyless entry device at a black Chrysler and the Chrysler beeped obediently. He opened the driver's door and slipped inside.

Casey ran to his own car. He would follow him. He laid the pizza on the passenger seat, stuck the Pepsi between his legs, and cranked his car, just as the Chrysler pulled away from the curb. Growlmaster Stō tried to get Eyes' attention, to lodge a protest, but Eyes were busy. They were locked in on the black Chrysler that was sitting at the stop sign ahead, its right turn signal winking at Casey with a come-hither cadence.

Chapter 77

When the knock on the door came precisely at eight, Andy was pleased. He liked prompt service, and he had ordered breakfast room service to be served at eight o'clock. Two poached eggs. Dry toast. Orange juice. Coffee.

"Just a minute," he called.

"Mr. Miller?" the voice beyond the door called back, and there was another knock.

"Yes. Coming. Just a minute, I said." He was dressed, except for his shirt. He didn't want to get it wrinkled, and he certainly didn't want to risk getting an errant bit of egg yolk on it. At the first knock, he toyed quickly with the decision to leave it off or to put the shirt on, then take it off again when the delivery person left. But now that it was definitely a male voice on the other side of the door, he decided not to put the shirt on. You never knew what was on the other side of the door—a dandy or a tiger. He knew how to strike a shirtless pose, if the situation warranted it.

He flipped back the latch, turned the security bolt, and opened the door. He was not at all prepared for the wild-eyed man who burst into the room.

Jock pushed the door closed behind him, and before the startled shirtless man before him could finish sputtering out his surprise, Jock pulled the Savage .32 and pointed it at him.

"Your wallet," he said and shoved the gun

forward to punctuate the demand.

"Don't hurt me," Andy gasped. He could feel his heart drumming in his chest. *Oh, my God, oh, my God, oh, my God*, he could hear himself squealing in his own head.

"I said gimme the fuckin' wallet!" Jock repeated. His eyes looked crazed. Andy wondered if the man was "on something."

"There," Andy pointed to the dresser. "Take it. Just take it and leave. *Please*."

On top of the dresser, his wallet, his money clip, his comb, his pocket change purse, and his keys were laid out in a precisely spaced row. He hadn't put them into his pockets yet. He hadn't wanted to spoil the lines of his trousers.

Jock snatched the wallet and the money clip and stuffed them into his pocket, apparently unconcerned with the unsightly bulge they created in his own trousers. Jock glanced around the room, and his gaze stopped at the bathroom door.

"Get in the bathroom," he said.

"What?! I don't—"

"I said get in the fuckin' bathroom! I'm not gonna tell you again!"

"Please," Andy begged, "please don't hurt me."

"Just get in the fuckin' john and lie down. Count to a thousand. And you better not come outa there before then." For emphasis, Jock reached over for the phone and yanked it. The cord snapped loose.

277

Andy backed into the bathroom. *Oh, my God, oh, my God, oh, my God*, he thought. *He's going to kill me. If I lie down, he's going to shoot me.*

As he half-turned, Andy's eyes fell on the Redken Rewind 06 Styling Paste. It was at the end of a meticulously arranged display of grooming products on the bathroom vanity. And something clicked in Andy's muscle memory.

There is no way to know, of course, who coined the term *coincidence*. Wouldn't it be just perfect, though, if it was the same guy who invented the phrase "coined the term"? Human beings are fascinated by coincidence. Observers of coincidence seem to fall into one of two camps: those who view it as some sort of mystical phenomenon; and those who see it as a quantifiable mechanistic inevitability.

To those with the mystic view, the idea is that every event has been or is being scripted in a giant cosmic Blue Horse notebook by some omniscient, divine puppet master. An old French proverb says: Coincidence is God's way of remaining anonymous. Believers point to things like, in Psalm 46, which just happened to be published in the same year that Shakespeare turned 46, the 46th word is "shake." Count backwards 46 words from the end and you come to—you guessed it—"spear."

The other camp touts science. Science explains coincidences statistically. Something that happens to only one person in a *billion* on any given day happens 2000 times a year. The whole thing is as supernatural as, say, long division.

While you meander over to the camp that is most to your liking, consider this. Redken Rewind 06 Styling Paste is marketed in a 5 ounce jar that has a circumference of 9 inches. A regulation baseball has a circumference of 9 inches and weights—yep—5 ounces.

Andy Miller felt his hand close around the jar. When he turned, it was with a pick-off move to first.

An object moving at 92 MPH travels 134.9 feet per second. The jar of Redken Rewind 06 Styling Paste that left Andy Miller's right hand traveled the nine feet to Jock Dejohnette's face in approximately seven-one hundredths of a second. Hardly enough time for any real debate about the philosophical aspects of coincidence. Certainly not enough time for Jock to react.

With small quantities of Redken Rewind 06, applied at normal salon speeds, one can "twist, shape, and texturize hair into changeable styles." An entire jar, applied at 92 MPH, will contort one's entire body into changeable styles that would make a Chinese circus performer say "Lawdy!"

The jar smacked Jock in the right cheekbone, just below his eye. His head snapped backwards, and his finger reflexively jerked the trigger as the pistol flew from his hand.

Andy's follow-through carried him to his

left, out of the doorway. The bullet smashed the bathroom mirror, and the gods immediately launched into a spirited debate about whose fault it was and who, therefore, was to be tagged with the seven year penalty.

Jock screamed, collapsed to his knees, and grabbed his face. Andy screamed and slammed the bathroom door. Jock pulled his hand back from his face, and his mind could make no more sense of the bloody, gelatinous goo smeared across his fingers than a chimp with a chemistry set. Was it snot? Eyeball jelly? Brain matter?!

The Savage .32 had slid across the floor and under the bed. Jock bolted for the door to escape. Andy ripped down the shower curtain rod, yanked it apart, and fiercely gripped a section of it like a baseball bat.

Jock flung open the hallway door just as the room service waiter was about to knock. Later, as the waiter tried to describe to the police what the man looked like who had sent both he and the breakfast cart crashing to the carpet, he would begin by saying, "Did ya ever see that old movie, *The Blob*?" Toward the end, he would say that as he lay on the floor, propped against the wall, and watched the door to the room close itself and click shut, he could hear a high-pitched male voice inside wildly shouting, "36!...37!...38!..."

Chapter 78

A bar. Of course it would be a bar that the black Chrysler parked in front of. The man got out, walked up to the door and knocked. The place wasn't even open yet. Someone inside apparently unlocked the door. The man pulled the door open, stepped inside, and let the door close behind him. Casey wondered if the door had locked.

He could wait, he told himself. *But, no,* he thought, *he probably works there. Might even own the place.* Why else would he be there like this, with the place closed? Someone else was inside, too, though. Did he really want to do this with somebody else there?

Casey looked at the name of the bar. The Strike Two. *What kind of name is that for a bar?* he wondered. He thought of Larry Lupo and Blackie Black. He was down two strikes himself. Time to step up to the plate and do it. He got out of his car and headed for the door of the Strike Two.

The door was slightly ajar. Casey pulled on it, and it opened. He stepped inside. It was so dim inside that it took several moments for his eyes to adjust. Before they had fully adjusted, someone spoke to him.

"We're closed."

It was a distinctly Brooklyn accent. Casey squinted, trying to make out the figure sitting at the end of the bar. He decided to gamble on the unlikelihood that Clifford Woodrow Zildjian spoke native Brooklynese.

"I was looking for—" he hesitated. *Don't make it too official-sounding*, he thought. "—uh, Mr. Zildjian."

"Yeah?" the voice replied—Casey could see him now; it was not the man he'd followed. "He's in the can. He expectin' you?"

"I don't think so," Casey answered.

"No? Well, like I said—we're closed. Why don' you come back when we're open?" The suggestion carried all the warmth of the soggy butt of the unlit cigar around which it was articulated. "What kinda business you got wit Woody? I'll tell 'im you was here."

Woody, Casey made a mental note. *Woody Zildjian.*

Taz sat at the bar and chewed his cigar. He was there to talk to Woody about a little business of their own. The liquor license was coming through. The lawyer that he and Tony used had drawn up some papers outlining the limits of Woody's share of the partnership. He would be a partner strictly in the Ball One enterprise, with no claim to or control in the other two establishments. He had placed his bet on Ball One, and he either made his investment back or lost it all on the success or failure of that one place. Taz didn't have time right now to be interrupted by some kid who came wandering in off the street looking for Woody.

"I'm, uh..." Casey paused, searching for the right line.

"Spit it out, kid," Taz stood up and started walking in Casey's direction. "Who're you? We're kinda busy here."

"I'm his son," Casey heard himself say. That wasn't the line he was looking for.

Taz' face instantly brightened into a smile— with a cigar butt stuck in its corner. He stuck out his hand, grasped Casey's hand in a firm grip, and smacked Casey on the right shoulder with his left hand.

"Why didn' ya say so? Jeez, ya come nosin' in here like some fuckin' creep off th' street, and—"

Woody appeared from the hallway at the other end of the room.

"Hey, Wood—" Taz announced. He spread his arms in a big *Ta! Da!* pose. "Look who's here! Why didn' you tell me your kid was here? I didn' even know you *had* a son!"

Woody stopped.

"I don't," he said.

This was not going the way he had it planned at all, Casey thought.

Taz turned back to Casey. The smile was gone.

"So who th' fuck're *you*, wiseguy?" Taz' left hand clamped onto Casey's right arm like a vice-grip, and he started pushing Casey backwards toward the door. Casey fought back the impulse to resist. He shouted, instead, toward the figure across the room.

"Does the name Katie Frye mean anything to

283

you?!"

The name came at Woody like a fastball.

"Wait!" Woody blurted.

Taz stopped, his hand still gripping Casey's right arm.

"How do you know Katie Frye?" Woody said.

"She's my mother," Casey answered.

In the silence that followed, the realization settled over Woody like a parachute floating down in slow motion and collapsing around him in a silky cocoon—that if this kid knew about Katie Frye and knew enough to connect Katie Frye with *him*, he knew everything.

Taz finally broke the silence.

"Somebody wanna let me in on th' joke or *what*?"

"It's okay," Woody said. "Let him stay."

Chapter 79

After he had shoved past the startled tourist and into the McDonald's restroom and looked into the mirror, what he saw seemed half Jock Dejohnette, half Charles Laughton's Quasimodo. Once he realized that he wasn't blind in his right eye, he washed off the bloody paste, dabbed at the cut atop his cheekbone with a piece of toilet paper, and he saw that he was going to have some shiner. *Fuckin' faggot*, he hissed.

Were he a blessings counting kind of guy, he would have offered thanks that the high-speed hair care projectile hadn't taken his right eye out, or knocked his front teeth down his throat, or crushed his larynx, but he wasn't much of a blessings counter. His take on things was more along the lines of, when you're drowning in shit, does it really matter whether you see the cesspool as half empty or half full?

It was clear that he couldn't do the purse thing today. Not looking like this. And the gun was gone. *Stupid cocksucker*, he seethed. He would have to lie very low for the rest of the day. But he had the wallet, the i.d. That was something. A start. And he had to get out of town. Soon. Tomorrow he would hit the purses. Tomorrow would be temp day. Temp day. Travel day. Tuesday. He could still make this work.

He looked at his right eye, purpling and swelling. *Shoulda killed the cocksucker*, said the voice in his head. It wasn't the Retributor talking. It was Jock.

Chapter 80

"Listen—" Woody said to Taz, "I'd consider it a favor if you'd let me have some time alone here with the kid. I'll tell you all about it later."

"Sure," Taz said. "If you guys leave before I get back, jus' lock up, okay?"

"Thanks," Woody nodded. "If you want to leave the paperwork, I'll take it with me and look it over later."

"No problem," Taz slapped Casey on the shoulder again as he headed for the door. "Make y'self at home, kid."

A shaft of bright light burst through the door as Taz exited. The door swung to and the dimness reclaimed dominion over the tableau in front of the bar.

Without a word, Casey walked slowly to within a few feet of Woody and stopped. They just looked at each other. For Woody, it was like looking at an old, life-sized photo of himself. For Casey, it was like gazing into a magic mirror that allowed you to see your future.

"So what's this about Katie Frye?" Woody finally spoke.

"You had an—" Casey stopped. He almost said *affair*. "—a romantic relationship with her."

"That was a long time ago. A different lifetime," Woody said.

"You never knew it—she never told you—but she became pregnant from that...time you spent together."

"She was married," Woody said. It wasn't a denial; he just said it matter-of-factly.

"Yes. She was. She had a baby. But it was your child. I am that child."

"You want a drink?" Woody asked, and he crossed around and behind the bar. "A cigarette? 'Cause I'm gonna have one. Both, actually. One of each."

"That's your response?!" Casey barked. "I tell you that you wrecked this woman's life—my *mother's* life!—my father's life—the man I *thought* was my father—*my* life—and that's all you have to say: You want a *drink*?!"

Woody poured himself a double shot of Ketel One over ice in an old fashion glass.

"If your life—' Woody paused and fished a cigarette from a pack behind the bar. "—I'm sorry; you didn't tell me your name." He waited.

"Casey. Casey Frye."

"If your life is wrecked, Casey Frye, I'm not sure I'm totally responsible for that. I mean, it's *your* life, and up until a few minutes ago, I don't believe I've had much at all to do with how you've lived it. So—yes—I'm having a drink. Would you like one?"

"No," Casey answered. "No, thank you."

"Suit yourself."

"What do you think—that I made this up? That I picked your name out of the phone book?"

"No," Woody said. He struck a match from a

pack on the bar and touched the flame to the end of the cigarette. "If you know about Katie Frye and me, I'd say you've gone to a whole lot more trouble than looking in the phone book. What I don't know is why. Why you're here. Why *are* you here, Casey Frye?"

"I needed to find my biological father," Casey began. He took a deep breath.

"Lots of people—when they think they've found out—"

Casey interrupted him. "I wasn't finished with what I was saying."

"Well...by all means, finish."

"I needed to find my biological father. Because I need a transplant."

"Oh," Woody said. He took a drink. "Oh," he repeated, because he wasn't sure what else to say. For several moments, neither of them spoke. "Sit down," Woody finally came up with. "Sit down and tell me the whole story."

Casey sat down on the bar stool opposite Woody.

"I'll take a beer, I guess," he said after a few moments. "I burned the roof of my mouth."

Chapter 81

Casey sat on the bed in his room at the Arlington and listened to the silence on his mother's end of the phone. He was talked out, having recounted to Katie the afternoon he had spent with Woody Zildjian. Katie had mainly just listened. Casey waited for her to say something.

"How does he look?" she asked quietly.

"It's almost spooky, Mom. It's like you said. He looks like an older version of me. It's kind of a weird feeling."

"I'd like to see the two of you together. I think."

"He has...a girlfriend, Mom. A *serious* girlfriend."

"What did you expect, Casey—that when you found him and introduced yourself that he and I would run slow-motion toward each other through a field of wildflowers, and bluebirds would dress me in a white wedding gown?"

"I don't know. I'm pretty sure I didn't picture bluebirds. Besides—" Casey hesitated a moment, "—I'm not sure I want him running toward you, at all."

"What does that mean?" she asked.

"I just don't think he's the kind of guy I'd like to see hanging around you, is all."

She laughed ever so lightly. "Well, thank you so much for screening any potential gentleman callers for me, sir."

"Mom...!"

"I'm just kidding, Casey. That's very sweet, actually." She paused. "So he's still something of a scoundrel, then, you think."

"Well..."

"That was always part of his allure, I think. Though I also think, for the most part, the 'bad boy' exterior was just that: exterior. For show."

Casey thought about the glimpses he had gotten of that rough exterior earlier that afternoon.

"Tell me about this cancer and transplant thing—just for laughs," Woody had said.

"For *laughs*?!" Casey stood up. He felt his hand tighten on the beer bottle. He had to stop himself from throwing it.

"Not for *laughs* laughs—sorry—that was the wrong way to put it. I just mean—you know— you've gone to all this trouble to find me. You might as well lay the whole thing out for me."

It was explanation, not contrition, but Casey sat back down. He just looked at Woody.

"So what's the deal on the transplant?" Woody asked.

"The *deal*?"

"Yeah. What kind of transplant are we talking about here?"

"Testicular."

"Testic—?"

"As in testicles."

"Testicles?"

"Testicle, actually. Just one."

291

"You want me to donate a *testicle*?"

"You have two."

"I *know* I have two! They're *my* testicles! I've counted them!"

He wasn't exactly a font of compassion and empathy. Katie's voice on the phone reeled Casey back to the present.

"So how did you leave it? Will the two of you talk again or what?"

"Um...yeah. Basically, he said I'd dumped a load on him and he needed some time to sort it all out. There was someone he wanted to talk to about it. That girlfriend, I think."

"Well, he didn't say 'no.' It sounds like it could have gone much worse."

"I guess."

"You did dump a load on him," Katie said quietly.

"I was just passing it on," Casey responded. "I wasn't the one who started stacking that ton of bricks."

Chapter 82

Merilee looked at Woody and thought, six months ago, if a man had told her the story that Woody had confessed to her last night, she would have brushed him off like white lint off of a little black dress. And now here he was topping last night's tale with another bizarre drama: an out-of-the-blue, grown son after one of his balls.

And yet, rather than running away as fast as her two shapely legs could carry her, she had this over-powering urge to hug the big galoot. For a moment, she felt a little like she figured Fay Wray must have felt after she realized that Kong liked her for more than just her bite-sized petiteness. She gave in to the urge —wrapped her arms around him, pressed her head to his chest, and squeezed.

"What's that for?" Woody asked.

"I've known people with some seriously fucked-up pasts, but I think you should win some kind of prize. And this was the best I could come up with at the moment."

"Thank you."

"You're welcome."

"Is this where you tell me you're just going to run up to the store for a pack of tampons and a frappuccino, and I never hear from you again?"

"I think you're confusing me with that girl who just thought you were a pretty good lay. ... Before you finagled yourself into that picture she has of the future. Remember?"

"Oh. ... *Pretty* good?"

"Okay—most satisfactory."

"Thank you."

"You're welcome."

"No—I mean, for saying that. The part about the picture."

"Remember that…when you're mounted and framed and hanging on the wall next to a picture of the two of us surrounded by my entire family at Glendi."

"Glendi?"

"Big gathering. Family. Friends. Food, drinks, dancing. Think 'Greeks Gone Wild'."

"Sounds like my kind of party. Assuming your family doesn't draw and quarter me for corrupting their little girl."

"Why, you haven't corrupted me even once today," she said in her best pouty little girl voice. "And you do it *most* satisfactorily."

"Today's not over," he bantered back.

"No—they'll love you. There's only one little thing we might have to worry about with the family."

"What's that?" Woody asked.

"You do realize that Zildjian is a Turkish name," she said.

"Ah," he nodded. They were both quiet for several moments. He looked at her and smiled. "Pick one you like," he said.

Chapter 83

With the recovery of the gun and the ballistics match to the bullet from Blackie Black's chest, the police knew that Jock was still in the city, and that he was still dangerous. At least he wasn't armed now. Not with the Savage .32, anyway. But he was clearly desperate—operating in Manhattan now and preying on tourists.

Detectives Thorn and Ring prepared BOLO (Be On the Look-Out) sheets on Jock Dejohnette for roll-call distributions in the midtown and lower Manhattan precincts, as well as in several precincts in Brooklyn. Detective Bozzone decided to drop some off at the Port Authority, also, in the World Trade Center.

Jock sat alone at a small formica-topped table in an eatery just down from the *Post* Building on Vesey Street. He was nursing a fountain Coke in a carry-out cup—alternately sipping and pressing the ice-filled cup to his still-swollen cheek. He was thinking about setting those bastards straight at the *Post*—letting them know who they had demeaned with their story. He had a CD with copies of the first three issues of *The Retributor* on it. He could drop it off with a note to the editor, show them that they were dealing with an artist and a champion of retributive justness. *Then* they'd see how wrong they were, how unfairly their rush to press had been, and how it had driven a man of justice to acts of desperation.

As he calculated and sipped and cooled his purple cheek, he sketched a scene on the back of a flier promising "$25/hr. Summer Jobs for Students."

In the first frame, a man on his knees, his hands bound behind him, gazed lustily at an erect penis that jutted from the left edge of the frame. In the second frame, the man appeared lost in the bliss of a no-hands blowjob to the penis—obviously several inches deep into his mouth, yet the shaft still extended to the left border of the frame. In frame three, the expression on the man's face had turned from lust to panic. His eyes were wide with terror and a bulge had developed at the base of his skull. The penis continued to drive forward from somewhere beyond the left outline of the frame. The final frame depicted the head of the penis and several inches of the seemingly endless shaft protruding through the back of the man's skull. The head of the penis erupted a flood of semen, which splattered against the right edge of the frame, as the head of the man exploded a chowder of brains and blood.

Jock wished he had a red pen.

He glanced at the clock on the wall. It was time to begin. There were purses to be picked. There were trains to be caught. The education of the idiot reporters at the *Post* would have to wait.

A short distance uptown, Andy Miller stood at a corner in the Village and tried to hail a taxi. He would be late, he thought, but he didn't much care.

He had sought solace from yesterday morning's trauma last night in way too much white wine and the arms of a gentle, soft-spoken, older man with an apartment on Charles Street. He glanced at his wristwatch and waved at another unseeing cabbie. *Oh, well,* he said to himself, *I'll never be invited back, anyway, I'm sure.*

Chapter 84

As Jock walked to the temp assignment location he had picked as his target, he thought of what he might say to anyone who asked about his black eye and swollen cheek.

Biking mishap, he thought. *Yeah,* he calculated, *I'll tell 'em I was riding in the park, and I swerved to miss a dog. People love dogs.* "Fuckin' mutts," he muttered to himself.

When he entered the lobby, he glanced at the clock on his way to the elevators. 8:25. *Perfect,* he figured, *I can work my way down five or six floors, and still be outa here before lunchtime. Hell, if I'm lucky, I can hit a purse or two while I'm still pretending to look for the personnel office.*

An elevator door opened, and after the car emptied, he stepped inside and moved over against the wall next to the button panel. While the car filled up with others on their way to another day at work, Jock opened one of the manila folders he was carrying—always carry manila folders, he had learned; it made you look like you were busy with something important—and he did a quick visual check of the temp paperwork he had already filled out. His name. Social Security number. Today's date: 09/11/01. Everything looked in order.

The last person squeezed his way into the car, and Jock pressed the button for his floor again. He would start with the 98th. The door closed, and the elevator began its climb up and up through the

North Tower of the World Trade Center.

Detective Tony Bozzone was cutting through the lobby when he caught a glimpse of the face, just as the elevator door was closing. *Damn*, he thought, *damn, if that didn't look like the sonuvabitch.* He considered the possibilities. No way to go looking for him. Too many places; too many faces. *Maybe I'll hang around outside for a while*, he thought to himself, *and see if he comes wandering back out.* He walked outside and sat on a bench and looked up at the two towers gleaming like the pillars of the Pearly Gate in the morning sun.

EPILOGUE

Dr. Strejc smiled as he left the room. Both of his patients were resting comfortably.

There was a meeting in progress on Casey's side of the room, in the corporate chambers of Testicle Central. Everyone knew there had been a major shake-up; they just weren't sure what that meant in terms of their future. Everyone was quiet as the boss began to speak.

"Obviously, the world is changing, and if we're going to survive, we're going to have to change with it. I know you're all confused— disoriented, maybe—what with being uprooted— the move to the new location. That's natural; it's understandable.

Now, I'm not going to stand up here and X and Y you to death. I'm going to give it to you straight. There's new blood among us. Some of you are already aware of this—feeling the effects. Even as I speak, we're getting in fresh shipments of brand new DNA. I know none of us have ever worked with this new material. We're having to do some re-tooling and re-training so that we can accommodate the new materials. But I've got confidence in you. We can do this.

I'll be honest with you—we're not sure what this is going to do—how it's going to affect the product line, how much it's going to change it. But one thing's for sure. It will change it. I, for one, believe it'll be a change for the better. Whole new possibilities, new markets for our product. I believe it'll add years to the life of our whole operation here.

Let us not forget—this old round world is all we've got. So let's go. Let's make this work!"

Across the room, Woody slept and dreamed. In the dream, he walked through a waterfall and, on the other side, discovered that he was standing and looking at what he instinctively knew was a better world. People everywhere turned and smiled and greeted him, as if they'd been expecting him.

"Hey, Sport!" a voice called to him, "Catch!"

It was his father. His old man threw a baseball to him. He caught it barehanded and looked at it. It was glistening white, perfect. He could feel the slightly raised seams of the red stitching.

"Look!" his father said to him. "It's autographed."

He turned the ball in his hand and read the bold black signature: *Lennie Lupo*. It was *his* handwriting.

THE END

Originally from Charlotte, North Carolina, Lew Holton now lives in the seaside community of Murrells Inlet, South Carolina. An award-winning playwright, his plays—including *Hand Jive, The Rapid Decline of Billy Ray Bouton, Gauguin Painting Paradise, Tomato Sandwich Simple, The Early Miracle, Reese and Babe,* and *Beer and Hypotheticals*, among others—have appeared on stages in New York and throughout the wider theatre world. His plays have been published by Palmetto Play Service, *Dramatics* magazine, *Southern Theatre* magazine, and Playscripts, Inc. His play *Portal* won the SETC 2004 Charles M Getchell New Play Award. He is also the author of *The Community Theatre Actors' Bible: 10 Secrets to Better Acting for Untrained Actors.* His first novel, *The Season of Preacher Jack,* was published in 2014.